ENEMY OF THE STATE

Security Services in the West are jittery with the renewal of the Cold War. Civilization has grown complex and vulnerable to an internal enemy. An act of sabotage could be unleashed on a massive scale — an atom bomb can be carried in a suitcase . . . This nightmare is realised when an enemy agent plants an atom bomb, set to detonate imminently. It must be located and deactivated, before thousands die and an entire town becomes radioactive ash . . .

E. C. TUBB

ENEMY OF THE STATE

Complete and Unabridged

LINFORD
Leicester

First published in Great Britain

First Linford Edition
published 2013

British Library CIP Data

Tubb, E. C.
    Enemy of the state. - -
    (Linford mystery library)
    1. Suspense fiction.
    2. Large type books.
    I. Title II. Series
    823.9′14–dc23

    ISBN 978–1–4448–1511–5

Published by
F. A. Thorpe (Publishing)
Anstey, Leicestershire

Set by Words & Graphics Ltd.
Anstey, Leicestershire
Printed and bound in Great Britain by
T. J. International Ltd., Padstow, Cornwall

This book is printed on acid-free paper

1

Enemy of the State

At the age of fifteen, Fred Yendle donated ten dollars to the Aid-Russia Fund and lived to regret it.

The fact was brought up as evidence against him five years later, when he was expelled from college. The reason for his dismissal was that he had been reading subversive literature; he had borrowed *Das Kapital* from the school library. The book, among others, was later withdrawn to save others from temptation, but by that time Fred had become mixed up with an abortive world peace movement whose membership consisted of equal parts of fellow travellers, intellectual communists and idealistic adolescents. He resigned after a few months, sick of the one-sided propaganda, but that didn't help him when he applied for security clearance so as to take up a minor post with the government.

The investigators turned him down flat, branded him as a suspected subversive and effectively damned him.

At the age of twenty-five he had married, a marriage which produced no children, no happiness and a divorce after eighteen months. Ten years later he was dismissed from his job as a clerical worker attached to a firm contracting for the government. He had worked in the same job for twelve years, handled nothing even remotely connected with defence, and so appealed to his union. The union held an inquiry, discovered that Fred had been discharged because he was considered a bad security risk, and promptly expelled him from the union. He appealed, the appeal was thrown out of court, and the costs effectively ruined him.

The next fifteen years followed the pattern in ever decreasing circles. Security had damned him, and Security, in importance, had become second only to God.

At the age of fifty, Fred Yendle arrived

in Alamushta with six hundred dollars, a three-day beard and one small suitcase.

He was a slight man, his shoulders stooped, his eyes weak, his suit baggy. He walked along the platform, the suitcase pulling him down one side, and his thin hair blowing in the desert wind. To most people he was a mild, inoffensive, rather pathetic figure. To the Security cop he was something to justify his existence. He stepped forward and barred Yendle's passage.

'All right, you. What have you got in that suitcase?'

'What?' Fred halted. 'Nothing much, just a few samples.'

'Open it up.'

'Why should I?' Fred took a tighter hold on the case. 'I'm doing no harm, just walking towards the restroom. No harm in that, is there? It's a free country, isn't it?'

'Sure,' said the cop. 'And we want to keep it that way. Now open up or I'll run you in — '

'What for?'

'Hampering Security in the course of

its investigations,' said the cop shortly. 'I want to see what's in that case.'

Fred hesitated, then, setting down the case, snapped the catches and opened the lid. 'I'm a traveller in electronic equipment,' he said. 'Transistor radios and tape recorders. This is a universal tape recorder. It will record, play back, sound-mix and blend at various speeds. The price is . . . '

'Save it,' snapped the cop. He stared at the neat layout in the case. Suspiciously, he turned a switch, listened to a burst of music, turned another and heard a businessman dictating a letter.

'I've got it loaded with tapes for demonstration purposes,' said Fred. He rubbed at his chin. 'I want to leave it here while I get shaved and cleaned up ready for an interview.' He looked at the cop. 'Can I go now?'

The Security cop nodded. He had no Geiger, no specialised knowledge, and thought, like most people, that a atom bomb was something as big as a ten-ton truck.

Fred shut the suitcase, picked it up,

continued his journey to the check-baggage section of the station. He inserted coins into a locker, opened it, put the suitcase into the metal cubicle, set the combination lock and slammed the door. He had paid for two days. At the end of that time, unless he either inserted more coins or removed the case, the locker would open and the contents be removed to the general depository.

He wasn't worried; two days was just one day more than he wanted.

Three hours later he was over four hundred miles away, at an airport waiting for a plane to take him over the border. There was a three-hour delay in the flight, and to kill time he entered the bar. He was sipping his third whisky sour when two men, dressed alike in slouch hats, raincoats and dark suits, walked up to him.

'Yendle, Fred Yendle?'

'That's right.' To deny it was useless. Everyone carried identification in these days. He produced his without being asked and handed it over. 'Police?'

'Security.' One of the men glanced at

the identification, nodded, and took Fred's arm. 'You're the man. Come along with us.'

'Why?' Fred knew, but something within him caused him to hang back. 'What do you want me for?'

'You're under arrest.'

Yendle laughed.

★　★　★

Doctor John Evans was listed as Civilian Expert, Interrogation Corps, and so was important enough to be flown fifteen hundred miles, but not important enough to be transported by military aircraft. He sat next to the window of the big skyliner, a young-old man, his hair shot with silver, his soft brown eyes seemingly capable of holding an infinite understanding. The receiver of a playback was clipped to his ear, the thin wire running to the recorder resting on the vacant seat beside him, and a heavy file of papers flattened his knees. Work and sleep were two things he just couldn't seem to fit within the twenty-four hours of each day. Usually sleep suffered.

The whispering voice in his ear stopped and he removed the receiver, made a note in his file, closed it and stared out of the window. Beneath him, the moving panorama of fields and roads, houses and small towns, hills and valleys made the countryside seem remote and almost toy-like. He found little to interest him in the view; his journey would last three hours and he had tired of it before it was a third over.

The stewardess, young, eager, artificially fresh, came down the aisle and halted beside him.

'Comfortable, sir?'

'Yes, thank you.' John glanced at her, recognising the routine behind the apparently sincere desire to please.

'Is there anything you require?'

'I don't think so.' John glanced through the window and felt a devil stirring within him. He pointed to where a pair of swollen-topped towers reared above a cluster of concrete buildings. Even from this height it was possible to see the fence surrounding the entire area. 'What are those buildings?'

'I'm afraid I don't know, sir.' She hadn't looked out of the window. 'Is there anything else? No? Don't hesitate to ring if you should need anything.' She smiled as she continued down the aisle and John returned the expression. He lost his smile as soon as he was alone.

It was no laughing matter.

It hadn't been a laughing matter for over twenty years now, and the war, the renewed cold war, naturally, though people no longer made that distinction, had grown steadily worse.

The spies and propaganda and underground cells could be tolerated; civilization had grown up with them as it had with cold and hunger and disease, but sabotage was something else.

Because a saboteur could, now, as never before, destroy a fantastic amount of material, production potential and man-hours of labour and time.

Civilization had grown unbelievably complex and that very complexity had made it hopelessly vulnerable to an internal enemy. A handful of grit could ruin the drive of battleship. A pair of clippers could rob an entire area of light and power and communications. A scrap of metal could derail a train, bring a factory to a halt or disorganize the smooth flow of supplies. Little things in themselves could have far-reaching consequences utterly out of proportion to the means used to create the disruption.

And an atom bomb could be carried in a suitcase.

It was impossible to forget that fact. One small bomb, correctly planted, could wreak more havoc than a hail of guided missiles from the skies. Propaganda had tried to deny it for fear of the repercussions on civilian morale, but the fact remained. One man, with one bomb, could cause more damage, at less cost, than any other weapon ever devised.

The defence was secrecy. Utter and absolute secrecy about anything and everything; justified in the name of Security and enforced with a desperate fanaticism born in hate and fear. No one knew anything about anything; they asked no questions and answered none. It was a natural result of the endless propaganda, security checks, loyalty checks and continual investigations which tried to ensure absolute loyalty and total security. They had failed. Sabotage had mounted and the hysterical insistence on Security had mounted with it. Now it had reached a stage where a man had to deny what his own intelligence taught him for fear of learning what he was not supposed to know.

And still the sabotage mounted.

John sighed as he thought about it. The stewardess had known as well as he did that the buildings with their unmistakable towers could be nothing other than an atomic reactor plant built at least twenty years ago. She had automatically denied that knowledge for fear of being accused, if anything happened to the plant, of subversive activities. What a person didn't know couldn't hurt them, and Security cops, uniformed and disguised, were everywhere. She probably thought that he had been trying to trap her.

He opened the file on his knees. It

contained the results of over two hundred investigations into various cases of sabotage, and, from them, he was working to crystallize the cause and so discover the cure for the trouble that plagued the nation. They ranged from an adolescent who had cut the phone wires serving an exchange so as to prevent his rival from calling up his girl friend, to a man who had deliberately overloaded the memory of a computer and so had ruined a valuable machine. From a line-repair man who had wanted more overtime, to a man who had used the mails to post letter-bombs to public figures against whom he had a grievance. Some were comic, some murderous, some stupid. Most were annoying rather than dangerous, and others were hopeless in their inefficiency. All were now punishable by death.

The stewardess came back down the aisle and gave John a strained smile. This time she didn't talk to him, and when he gestured, her smile became even more strained.

'Yes, sir?'

'I'd like some coffee, please.'

'Certainly, sir.' Her relief was pathetic. 'Anything else?'

'Yes.' He paused just long enough to make her unhappy. 'How long until we land?'

'Thirty minutes, sir. I'll get your coffee right away.'

* ★ *

The airport glistened in a wet drizzle, which made the security posters seem even more garish and tasteless than ever. Aside from the usual terse commands to *Button Your Lip! If You Know — Don't Tell!* and *Talk is Trouble!* there were others, apparently for those who could not read. A leering Mongolian with an exaggerated ear listened to a couple of well-dressed businessmen, a simian Oriental stabbed a beautiful girl in the back, a coffee-coloured head-hunter bared filed teeth at the spectacle of a burning city. All the representations were ludicrously distorted and would have been comic had the intent behind them not been so serious.

'Do they really work?' John glanced at the young officer who had met him. Mark Weston, his uniform bearing the insignia of the Interrogation Corps, hesitated before replying.

'If they can persuade one individual to take Security a little more seriously, then they have justified their existence.'

'A nice, safe answer,' said John. 'But what about the other effects? To portray as obscene enemies those who have different features or coloured skins to ourselves is hardly the way to prepare for world peace, is it?'

'I wouldn't know,' said Mark shortly. 'We can worry about that when the time comes.' In the car, he grew more friendly. 'I've heard about you, doctor, and of the fine work you've done in interrogation techniques. Your recommendations have been accepted as standard pre-interrogation procedure for all suspects.' He produced non-carcinogenic cigarettes, offered them, and lit them from a lighter. 'Would it be in order to ask if you are engaged on anything at the present?'

13

'The usual problem.' John inhaled, the smoke burning his throat. 'Sabotage, and what we can do to prevent it.'

'Doesn't that concern Security more than us?'

'Perhaps; Security would say so, I know. But Security tries to prevent sabotage by guarding essential installations and an ineffectual system of weeding out suspected persons.'

'Ineffectual?' Mark sounded slightly shocked. 'I would hardly call it that.'

'Why not? The proof is in the constant rise of sabotage. If the methods used by Security were as effective as they would have us think, then surely sabotage would drop, not mount.' John glanced out of the windows at the rain-swept landscape. They were travelling along a narrow, concrete road towards a grim, fortress-like building. 'This is just a theory, of course, but I feel that we are doing something wrong somewhere. Security is, in effect, locking the door after the horse has gone. You have probably noticed how, after each incident, Security clamps down a little tighter. Sometimes I wonder where it will all end.'

'It will end when the war ends,' said Mark shortly. 'Until then we must do the best we can.' He leaned forward as the car swept to a halt before a guard house. 'Captain Mark Weston returning with Doctor John Evans and driver.'

The guard stared through the windows of the car, made a note on a clipboard, then gestured the driver to continue.

Mark didn't resume the conversation and John had the uneasy feeling that he had said too much. Security was a brittle egg, and no one felt safe in even discussing it. Such talk could be twisted to mean dissatisfaction, and that could lead to an investigation. No one had ever come out of such an investigation with the same or higher security rating and, for a man depending on government work for a living, that was serious. Suspicion had a habit of snowballing, and once a man had been even remotely under a cloud he usually wound up in the gutter.

Government employees, like Caesar's wife, had to be above suspicion.

The car halted for a second time at the door of the fortress and Mark led the way into the building. John followed him, clutching his personal baggage, then had to wait while it was examined, his papers checked, and a phone call made to someone in the higher echelons.

'Routine,' said Mark, as he led the way to an elevator. 'All incoming personnel and baggage have to be cleared by Security.' The doors shut behind them, the elevator whined as it carried them up to the tenth floor, the doors opened and they halted before an armed guard. John patiently allowed his papers to be examined for the second time.

'The colonel will give you a twenty-four hour clearance for this building,' said Mark as they continued down a corridor. 'It'll make things a lot easier.'

'I see what you mean,' said John dryly, as they halted for the third time. 'From the look of things you must need Security permission in order to wash your hands.'

'We've got to be careful,' said Mark. 'I'll admit that it seems to be overdoing things, but it's better to be safe than sorry. Anyway, no loyal citizen should protest at regulations designed for the common good.'

'Of course not.' John returned his identification to his pocket. 'Who is in charge of Interrogation here?'

'Colonel Malcome. We are going to see him now.' Mark chuckled. 'This case has got him beat, but he'll tell you about it himself.' He paused before a door, knocked, waited, then opened it and stepped inside.

Colonel Malcome was a big man with a thick neck and hands that looked as if they could snap a two by four as though it were a match. His hair was short cropped and iron grey, his eyes a frosty blue, his mouth a thin crease above his chin. He waved John and Mark to chairs, continued reading a document before him, signed it, pushed it to one side, then turned his frosty eyes on John.

'I requested Interrogation Centre to send me an expert,' he said. His voice matched the rest of him: deep, harsh, impatient. 'I had expected an officer, not a civilian.'

'The lack of military rank gives me certain advantages,' said John smoothly. 'It makes it easier for me to gain the confidence of suspects and, when dealing with the military, I am unawed by superior rank. It makes things much easier if I can operate without the fear of being court-martialled and, from your point of view, anything I do cannot reflect on your organization.' He smiled. 'Anyway, does it matter?'

'As long as you can do your job, no.' Malcome dismissed the question as unimportant. 'Has Captain Weston briefed you?'

'No.'

'The position is this,' said Malcome. 'We have a suspect. We picked him up five hours ago and have treated him according to the general directive.' His tone left no doubt as to his private opinion of the blanket instruction that all suspects were to be brought to an Interrogation Centre, isolated, and treated more like delicate guests than the enemies of the State they usually were. John recognised the tone, the reason for it and the frustration behind it.

'The directive is based on common sense,' he said mildly. 'If the suspects are proven innocent, then they leave full of praise for Security and more law-abiding than ever. If guilty, then it doesn't really matter how they are initially treated, does it?'

'Doctor Evans is the man who recommended the general directive,' said Mark hastily. Malcome wasn't impressed.

'I consider it a waste of time,' he said coldly. 'But let us not go into that. Yendle has been under arrest for five hours now. I could have got the truth out of him in one.'

'But you tried, didn't you?' John smiled, but his eyes did not. 'You tried and failed, and so have made my task just that much more difficult.'

'I don't see that.'

'It is always more difficult to impress a man if he is convinced that you are a fool,' said John. 'On the other hand, it is always dangerous to underestimate your enemies.' This time, when he smiled, his eyes joined in. 'Let us say that the whole thing cancels out, shall we?'

'We passed the suspect through the normal pre-interrogation routine,' said Mark quickly, before Malcome could speak. 'Security has checked him and forwarded his dossier. We sent for you only when it became obvious that an expert was essential.'

'Any traps?'

'None, he was clean.'

'Hypnosis?'

'Yes. I tried the usual routine, but the reactions were so violent that I had to desist.'

'And then?' John smiled as he waited for an answer. 'And then,' he continued, 'the Colonel grew impatient and tried more direct methods. He shouted and raved and probably threatened. He may even have appealed to the man's sense of decency and loyalty, and, of course, he achieved precisely nothing. Am I correct?' He didn't need an answer; their expressions confirmed what he had said. John sighed, the pattern was all too familiar. Call in the expert after everything else had been tried. 'I suppose that there is no doubt as to his guilt?'

'None.' The colonel turned his frosty eyes on the doctor. 'We know that he has committed sabotage, and he knows that we know it. We can even guess what manner of sabotage it was, but we don't know where, or when, or how. We won't know until it blows up in our face or until he tells us.'

'When you say 'know' do you mean that literally?'

'Yes. One of our agents passed us a list of names, and Yendle's was among them. We picked him up at an airport five hours ago.' Malcome frowned. 'He didn't struggle or attempt to escape. He seemed to regard the whole thing as a great joke.' The big hands clenched. 'I'll give him joke, the swine! He was hot when we checked him. His clothing and skin carried a high degree of radioactivity, far above anything that he could have picked up normally. Do I have to tell you what that means?'

'No,' said John. He felt a cramping of his stomach. It had come, the bomb in a suitcase, and for the first time he could sympathize with the colonel's impatience.

'How much time have we got?'

'How do I know? We are combing every possible area in which he could have been, back-tracking his movements and checking his associates. From the radioactivity on his clothing, he must have planted the bomb not more than twelve hours before his arrest, but that doesn't help. In twelve hours a man could go around the world.' Malcome picked up a thick dossier from his desk and handed it to John.

'Here is the dossier. Captain Weston will work with you and give you what help you may need.' He looked at John, 'Yendle has information. I must have that information. The lives and safety of I don't know how many people depend on my getting it. Your task is simple — make him talk.'

The way he said it made it sound easy.

★ ★ ★

Fred Yendle sat on a chair designed to give the maximum amount of discomfort in a room that was little more than a cell.

The door was set flush with the wall; in one corner high against the ceiling, the grille of an air conditioner matched the smaller one of a speaker. The two long walls were panelled with some dull grey material. The smaller wall opposite the door held a toilet. It, the door, the chair and floor and walls were all of the same uniform, neutral grey. It should have been restful, but all it did was to turn attention back on itself.

But Yendle wasn't worried.

He hadn't been worried for a long time now, not since the moment when he had planted the suitcase at . . . He smiled. Best not to think of that name, best to think of anything but that name. Better even to think of his arrest than where he had planted the suitcase.

He had enjoyed the arrest. It had been so funny, so riotously amusing, the two men so serious, the hand on his arm, the startled expressions of those around him, the whole thing added up to one big laugh. He chuckled as he thought about it, jerking up from his chair as the need for action overpowered him, and striding about the room with quick, jerky steps. He felt wonderful. He felt as if he could laugh and sing and jump in the air from very joy.

He did.

Mark scowled through the sheet of one-way glass separating the tiny office from the cell, then looked at John.

'He's at it again.'

'Is he?' John lifted his head and stared through the window. He sat at the desk, the dossier open before him, the thin sheets which comprised a man's life neat in their folder. 'Tell control to step up the carbon dioxide. He can't keep it up much longer.'

Mark nodded and picked up a phone. He relayed the order, listened, spoke again and hung up. 'Read that dossier yet?'

'Yes.' John closed the file and stared thoughtfully at Yendle. He had sat down again and seemed to be having trouble with his breathing. 'You say that he was clean?'

'We stripped, washed, X-rayed and examined him,' said Mark. 'No hidden poisons, weapons, planted bombs or bacteria. We made very sure of that.'

He sounded grim, and John knew what he was thinking. Saboteurs had long passed the stage where they were merely an instrument of destruction. Now, quite often, they were weapons in themselves, and too many interrogators had died as the result of surgically planted explosives.

'At least he is not a fanatical agent,' mused John. 'An enemy national would have taken full precautions against arrest. He resisted hypnosis?'

'Yes. I tried the usual techniques, but none of them worked. I tried a minimum dose of neoscop and he almost died.' Mark looked worried. 'Frankly, doctor, I don't know what else to do.'

'How did the colonel make out?'

'As you said. Yendle just laughed at us. He wasn't even worried when the colonel threatened immediate execution.'

'Naturally, he knew it to be an empty threat.' John glanced through the window again. 'What do you think of him, captain?'

'He's a traitor.'

25

'Is he?' John sighed. 'To you a traitor, to another, a patriot, to a third a misguided fool, to a fourth a tool to be used, to a fifth a man to be pitied. Who is right?'

'Do you pity him?'

'To me he is a problem,' said John. 'A safe to which I must find the combination, a puzzle which has to be solved, an adversary in a complicated game. Hate has no place in that game, nor fear, nor the desire to hurt. That is why we have an Interrogation Corps. The obtaining of information from suspected enemy agents, subversives and saboteurs is now a science.'

'Yes,' said Mark. He looked at John with an odd expression. 'You know, to listen to you, anyone would think that you sympathized with Yendle. You seem to forget what he is.'

'Every man is the result of what is done to him by others,' said John mildly. He nodded towards the window. 'Look at him, a normal seeming man, the kind of man you would imagine to have a home, wife, children. The kind of man who tends his garden, walks his dog and swaps garden-fence politics with his neighbours. And yet he's guilty of the basest crime we recognise.'

'The worst crime there could possibly be,' corrected Mark. 'There can be no excuse for treason.'

'That is a matter of opinion,' said John. 'Personally, I regard a man or woman who ill-treats their young as being worse than a traitor. Society can defend itself, a child cannot, but, naturally, you cannot agree with me.'

'Cannot?' Mark looked puzzled. 'I don't quite understand what you mean.'

'Forget it.' John concentrated on the papers before him, conscious of his own desire to hit out against a system he secretly despised, and yet knowing that attacking the end-products of the system was worse than useless. The captain could no more help his feelings than he could control the beating of his heart.

Beyond the window, Yendle rose, yawned, and walked about the narrow confines of the room. He yawned again, shook his head and resumed his seat.

'Better fetch him in,' said John. 'And tell control to restore the cell atmosphere to normal. We don't want him passing out on us.'

Yendle was enjoying himself. It was obvious from the way he acted, the manner in which he moved, the constant, almost hypnotic, flickering of his eyes. He smiled as John gestured towards a chair, and smiled even wider at the offer of a cigarette.

'What's all this, the all-old-pals-together act?' His voice was high-pitched and the words had a tendency to run together.

'I'm a smoker,' said John mildly. 'It would be rude of me to smoke alone; also,' he became confidential, 'your smoking gives me an excuse to indulge.' He lit both cigarettes, inhaled and stared at the suspect. 'Want to tell me about it, Fred?'

Yendle grinned, dragged at his cigarette, then stared at Mark, who had taken a chair just behind him. 'What about the boy scout, doesn't he smoke?'

'To hell with him,' said John. 'Forget him; he won't bother us.' He leaned

28

forward across the desk. 'Look, Fred, I'm a civilian, just like you, and you can talk to me. Now, why don't you just tell me all about it?'

'All about what?' Yendle's eyes halted in their flickering. 'I don't know a thing. I was just standing in the bar having a drink when those two goons came up to me and arrested me. All I was doing was waiting for my plane when they grabbed me. I don't know a thing.'

'Where were you going?'

'Mexico. I . . . '

'Why?'

'Why?' Yendle blinked, his spate of words halted by the abrupt questions. 'Why not? I can go to Mexico if I like, can't I? It's a free country, isn't it?' He sneered, his face becoming ugly. 'Like hell it is!'

'So you don't know a thing? Is that it?'

'That's right.'

'You mean that you were used? That you didn't know what you were doing?'

'I didn't say that. I knew what I was doing all the time, and I was glad to do it to those lousy cops . . . ' Yendle broke off and bit his lips. 'I'm not talking.'

'But you want to talk, don't you?' John smiled. 'You can't help it. You're full of words, they bubble inside you like the gas in a bottle of mineral water, and they want to come out.' His voice deepened and became infinitely persuasive. 'You don't have to be afraid of me, Fred. I'm your friend. You can tell me all about it. I've been through the mill myself and I know what it's like. Why not tell me about the party?'

'What party?'

'The hypkick party.' John was taking a chance, but it was worth the risk. 'I know all about them; been to a couple myself. What did they use, mirrors?'

'No, some . . .'

'Or maybe they used some revolving gimmick fixed to the lights.' The chance had paid off. John smiled as if at a pleasant memory. 'I remember one party I went to. Man what a night that was!'

'You're telling me!' Yendle's grin threatened to split his face. 'You don't know half. You want to go real deep, throw off those old inhibitions and hit bottom. You can't manage it the first time, but take a couple of pills and . . . '

John sighed, relaxing in his chair, only half aware of what the other was saying. Not that it mattered; the recorders would be saving every word, but he knew that the rush of words held little of importance.

It was arrest-euphoria, the near hysteria caused by post-hypnotic conditioning and triggered by the shock of arrest. Yendle, despite the depressive effects of the carbon dioxide pumped into his cell, was feeling on top of the world and so supremely confident of himself that nothing could touch him. Threats, to him, were unreal, everything was unreal. He was like a man high on a merry drunk and all he wanted to do was to talk and talk and talk. But he didn't talk about what John wanted to know.

The rush of words died and John, waiting for the moment, asked a question.

'Where did you plant the bomb, Fred?'

'Al . . . ' Yendle gulped, his face turning a dirty white and the words strangling in his throat. 'No!'

'Who gave you the bomb, Fred?'

'I can't tell you! I can't!'

'When is it due to blow, Fred?'

'I don't know!' Yendle recovered himself. 'You're wasting your time, you'll get nothing out of me.'

'No?' John shrugged. 'Don't be too sure of that, Fred. I won't hurt you, but others may. You know what they could do to you, Fred? They could give you a prefrontal leucotomy; they'd take an ice-pick and push it past your eye into your skull and rip the front part of your brain. It wouldn't kill you, Fred. It wouldn't even blind you, but you wouldn't be much of a man afterwards.'

'Hogwash!'

'Or they could experiment on you,' said John softly. 'They could take you and fill you with bugs so that your flesh would rot and stink, and you couldn't stand the sight of yourself. Or . . . '

'Cut it out,' said Yendle. 'You can't scare me.'

'I'm not trying to scare you.' John shook out fresh cigarettes and lit them. 'I'm just telling you what could happen to you. That bomb you planted was an atomic one. Did you know that?'

Yendle remained silent.

'They don't like that, Fred,' continued John. 'They want to take you out and work on you.'

'They won't kill me.' The conviction in his voice was incredible.

'Did I say anything about killing you?' John dragged at his cigarette until the tip shone bright red. 'Do you know what pain is, Fred? Real pain, I mean, the kind of pain that twists your nerves and seems to go on forever. You couldn't stand that sort of pain, Fred. You'd whine and beg and pray for them to kill you. And they could set up mirrors so that you could see what they were doing to you. You'd see them open your flesh and fish for a nerve, and when they touched it, it would double you up. But you wouldn't be able to move, Fred, you'd be strapped down on the operating table, and all you could do would be to look and scream, and scream, and scream. You'd have to tell them then, wouldn't you, Fred? But then it might be too late to save you. Why not tell me now and save yourself all that trouble?'

'Who are you kidding?'

'You don't believe me?' John leaned forward, reached out with his left hand and caught hold of Yendle's wrist. He pressed the glowing tip of his cigarette against the trapped hand.

Yendle fainted.

*   *   *

Colonel Malcome scowled at the map fastened against the wall, stabbed at it with a thick forefinger, then spun in his chair to glare at John.

'Al,' he said. 'Is that all you can get?'

'Yes. We've other information, of course, but nothing directly affecting the search. Are you working on it?'

'Naturally, but we can't work miracles. Just how many places do you think have names beginning with the letters Al?' Malcome snorted. 'There are thousands of them. Towns, states, installations, whistle stops and tank towns.' His finger jabbed towards the map again. 'We've

34

drawn a circle at the approximate range a man could normally travel in twelve hours. We've had to discount the skyliners and direct expresses; they cover the whole country. Even taking it at its lowest, the circle is a thousand miles in diameter, and it should be twice that to do a thorough job.'

'You can eliminate quite a bit,' said John. 'South of the border, the desert, the too-small towns and place-names. They wouldn't waste an atomic bomb on anything relatively unimportant.'

'Security's computers are working on that,' said Malcome. 'They are concentrating on essential installations in order of importance. The first search produced five localities within the area. They lowered their specifications and the second search came out with fifty-three. They are working on the third now.'

'Tough,' commented John, and knew that he was making a classical understatement. Each locality would have to be checked by Security, and each locality, in itself, was a full-sized job. The search had to be thorough, and, to be effective, would have to cover about five square miles of terrain. Even with the latest scintilloscopes it was a task to stagger the imagination, especially as most of the localities would be normally radioactive from the work done within them.

'It's more than tough,' said Malcome bitterly. 'It's impossible. Even assuming the letters Al designate the name of a specific locality, and not a state or place name it is impossible. Security just hasn't that amount of men to conduct the search. All we can do is to take a few at a time and work down the line and hope we reach it before it blows.' His big hands knotted into fists. 'And we don't even know how much time we've got.'

'No.'

'Can't you get it out of him?'

'Eventually, perhaps, but when is something else.' John lit a cigarette. 'He's unconscious now. I tested his pain level and found it, as I suspected, incredibly low. We shot some sedatives and something to lift the pain level into him, put him back in a vitiated atmosphere, and Mark is waiting for him to recover.' John stared at the thin coil of smoke rising from between his fingers. 'I found out that he had been to a hypkick party, probably more than one. I'd say that was where they first started indoctrinating him.'

'They should be stamped out.' Malcome sounded disgusted. 'A lot of perverts getting together to give themselves a lift from hypnotic illusions. Those parties are worse than dope.'

'I agree.' John held no brief for the illegal hypkick parties in which a hypnotist used a simple technique to induce trance and temporary illusions of grandeur. They were illegal, yes, but so was gambling, dope and pornography and no one, yet, had found a way of making the laws banning any of those things stick. The only way was to compromise, allow them to exist under semi-official supervision, but it was as impossible to control them as it had been to control drinking during prohibition.

An aide entered the office, saluted, dropped a paper on desk, saluted again and went out. Malcolme picked up the flimsy, read it, crushed it in his hand and flung it into the disposal bin. There was a brief flash as the paper was reduced to ash.

'The third run produced a hundred and eighty-seven localities,' he said. 'They're working on the fourth now. God knows how many they will get the next time.' He sounded desperate. 'Can't you blast the information out of him? Probe his mind or something?'

John shook his head,

The phone rang and Malcome scooped it up in one big hand. He listened, grunted, handed it to John. 'Captain Weston. He wants to speak to you.'

'Evans here.' John listened to the thin voice in his ear. 'No. He's had too much already. There's nothing we can do now until he snaps out of it. Let me know when he recovers consciousness.' He hung up and met the colonel's frosty blue eyes. 'Captain Weston is getting impatient,' he said. 'He wanted to try shock therapy.'

'Is that bad?'

'It could be fatal.' John picked up his

cigarette, drew on it, frowned, crushed it out and lit another. 'Look at it this way, colonel. If a guided missile were to land without exploding you would naturally investigate it. You would assume that it was a bomb, which could be detonated by any one, or more than one, of a number of fuses. Your expert would first have to determine what those fuses were, find some way to by-pass them, and then dismantle the bomb and find out what was inside. Fred Yendle is no different, in principle, to such a bomb. He has the knowledge we need but that knowledge is protected by mental and physical fuses which, if wrongly tampered with, will send it beyond our reach.'

'I follow you,' said Malcome. He was a single-minded man, but not an unintelligent one, and he had had experience of saboteurs before. 'The trouble is the time element. If he were an ordinary saboteur you could take all the time you want, but this time we can't give you that. The bomb he planted could blow at any moment.'

'I know it,' said John. 'It doesn't make

things easier.' He sucked smoke deep into his lungs, held it, let it stream through his nostrils. 'We know that Yendle is loaded with post-hypnotic commands. The arrest-euphoria proves that, as well as the refusal to be hypnotized. Hypnotic drugs caused a violent physical reaction, psychosomatic, of course, but nonetheless real or dangerous because of that. Further use of neoscop or other truth drugs will lead to a paroxysm resulting in death. He has also been protected against the third degree. His pain level was so low that he automatically fainted at the pain from a minor burn.'

'A nice picture,' said Malcome, and the lines in his face deepened as he thought about it. 'We can't beat the truth out of him; he will escape into unconsciousness at the first blow. We can't hypnotize him; he has been conditioned against it. We can't drug him; he will die.' The big hands clenched. 'Execution?'

'Not if you want the information. Yendle is a national, he has been reared in a law-abiding atmosphere, and he knows that you can't execute him without a trial.

He also knows that you won't kill him, because, if you do, you will lose the very thing you are trying to get.'

'But he doesn't expect to get away with this?' Malcome sounded incredulous. 'He must know that the penalty for sabotage is death. Surely, he doesn't think that he is going to walk out of here a free man.'

'Yes,' said John slowly. 'That is exactly what he does think.' He shrugged at the colonel's expression. 'Yendle isn't normal, and I'm speaking in the broadest psychological sense. His reactions are all wrong and totally artificial. He has no sense of guilt, no fear, no lack of confidence. He is unable to regard what he has done as serious. To him all this is a game. He has never seen a dead man, the shocking results of atomic disruption, the blood and wounds and shattered bodies. Basically, all he wanted to do was to cause trouble.'

'Trouble!' Malcome sounded grim. 'I'll give him trouble. I've got every man I can spare on the job. Every department of Security has been alerted and special groups of men flown out to those locations with the highest priority. Every installation selected by the computer has gone on full-security search. The loss of production alone must run into the millions of man-hours. And you talk of trouble.' The big hands clenched, matching the anger in the frosty eyes. 'I'll show that rat what trouble really means. Personal trouble.'

'Yendle will die,' said John evenly. 'You know it, I know it, but Yendle himself refuses to believe it. He is armoured in his conditioning, which has convinced him that nothing unpleasant can happen to him — providing he does not talk! Once he talks his protection has gone. To him, his silence is literally his life. If we try to blast it from him against his will he will fight against us in the only way he can. He will escape into insanity or unconsciousness. He may even escape into death.'

'I wouldn't call that much of an escape.'

'Psychologically speaking, death offers the perfect escape,' explained John. 'It is extreme, but it is always there. I need only mention suicidal mania to illustrate my point. But Yendle need not die to escape from us; he can always retreat. He can, mentally, return to the past, away from the troubles of the present. But no matter how far he retreats, he will always find troubles to escape from. He will retreat to the embryonic stage, unable to eat, to concentrate, to do anything to help himself. He will lie, curled up in the foetal position, utterly useless and absolutely helpless. We call it dementia praecox.'

'Nasty,' said Malcome. 'But not as nasty as a bomb tearing the heart from one of our cities. Yendle is only one man, a traitor at that, and he is expendable. What happens to him is not important; discovering the location of the bomb is.'

The phone rang and John arrested his instinctive gesture towards it. Malcome lifted the handset, listened, replaced it. 'That was Captain Weston. Yendle has recovered.' He looked grim. 'Don't be gentle with him, doctor. We need that information.'

★ ★ ★

Yendle had been arrested at 14.00 hours. He had been under arrest for five hours when John had arrived. The initial interview, the preparation and testing of the suspect had taken four hours. Yendle had been unconscious for ninety minutes. John had a mounting uneasiness that time was running out. He stared grimly at the suspect.

Yendle was no longer enjoying himself. The discomfort of the room, the vitiated air, the drugs injected into him had all worked to reduce his euphoria. A red patch on his cheek where Mark had slapped him seemed to cause him trouble. He kept touching it, shocked that he had felt the pain and had not lost consciousness. This time, when John offered him a cigarette, he took it more as a man thankful for small favours than with his previous air of cocky condescension.

'All right, Fred,' said John. 'Now I want you to talk. I'm not going to ask you where you planted the bomb, so you don't need to watch your answers.' He smiled. 'Let's make a game of it. If you answer, then I'll chalk up a mark. Ten marks and you get a cigarette. If you don't answer, then Captain Weston will hit you.' His smile became wider. 'You can't run away from the pain now, Fred, and it will hurt. When is the bomb due to blow?'

'I don't know.'

Mark stepped forward, his hand lifted. John shook his head.

'You mean that, Fred? You really don't know?'

'That's what I said.'

'Good, one mark. Who gave you the bomb?'

'I don't know. I mean it,' said Yendle hastily. 'I don't know. I picked it up from a check-baggage depository.'

'When?'

'Late last night.' Yendle looked bewildered. 'I think it was last night.'

'At what time?'

'About ten.'

'Where?'

'Houston, Texas. It was in one of those transient depositories at the bus station on Baynard Avenue.'

'What did you do then?'

'I caught a train.'

'To where?'

'To . . . ' Yendle hesitated, then cringed as Mark came towards him. 'I can't remember. I . . . '

Mark swung his hand.

It wasn't pretty and it wasn't nice, but it had to be done. John watched impassively as the captain slapped Yendle with a vicious one-two to either cheek. The blows, in themselves, were not too serious, but the mental effect they were having on the suspect was equivalent to a psychic explosion. He could be hurt. He didn't want to be hurt. The only way he could stop being hurt was to talk — but he dared not answer the question.

He compromised. 'To Albuquerque.'

'Albuquerque!' Mark halted the down-swing on his hand. 'Doctor, we've got it!'

John refused to be excited.

'Then what did you do?'

'I walked around for a while and then caught another train.'

'To where you were arrested?'

'Yes.'

'How much was the fare from Houston to Albuquerque?'

'I . . . ' Yendle swallowed. 'Fifty dollars.'

'What time did you arrive?'

'At dawn.' Yendle volunteered more information. 'I had breakfast at a diner and looked around before catching my train.'

'Is that where you left the bomb?'

'I . . . ' Yendle hesitated. 'Yes.'

'Where did you leave it?'

'In . . . ' Yendle swallowed, his adam's apple bobbing in his throat. 'In the cloakroom of a hotel.'

'Which hotel?'

'The . . . the Grand.'

'I see.' John picked up the phone, rang control, spoke, listened, replaced the receiver. 'You're lying, Fred, and you know it. You don't know the fare from Houston to Albuquerque, no train arrives at dawn, and there is no Grand Hotel.' He nodded to the captain and Mark stepped forward.

Yendle began to cry after the third blow.

John recognized the symptoms and halted the punishment. To continue it was worse than useless. No simple system of trick questioning would yield the desired information, and lies only wasted time. Yendle was willing to tell the truth only because the strain of remaining totally silent was too great for him. He had compromised with himself; the essential information he would retain, the rest he would divulge. He was like a man on a long hike who wanted to lighten his load. He would dispense with everything but the one item necessary to his survival. His lies were merely a protective device to save him from punishment. Continue the punishment and he would find escape in some other way.

John reached for the phone, called the colonel, gave him the news.

'He either slept next to the bomb or travelled with it on the seat beside him,' he said. 'That would account for the radioactivity on his skin and clothing. Does that help you at all?'

'No,' said Malcome. 'With transport the way it is he could have travelled fast or slow, direct or by a circular route. But I'll put men onto checking all transport leaving Houston during the effective period.' John heard him suck in his breath. 'But it takes time! Time!'

'That's another point,' said John. 'The delay between the planting of the bomb and the blow-up seems all wrong. The only way I can account for it is to assume that it could not have been planted later than it was. What localities have you that enforce a total Security ban at set periods? If there are any, then maybe we can isolate the bomb that way.'

'I'll work on it,' said Malcome. 'Let me know if you get anything new.'

John hung up, reached for a cigarette, and suddenly met the eyes of Yendle. The official in him gloried at the dull beaten expression in his eyes.

Pity made him hand the man a cigarette.

★　★　★

Mark opened the door, took something from someone outside, closed the door and returned to the desk with a tray bearing cups and coffee.

'White or black?'

'Black, with plenty of sugar.' John turned from where he had been staring at Yendle through the one-way glass. It was 03.00 hours, the suspect had been returned to his cell an hour ago, and John was beginning to feel the full effects of fatigue. His head ached a little, his eyes seemed full of grit and his mouth burned from too much smoking. He had been awake most of the previous night working at his papers and now missed the lost sleep. How Yendle must feel was anyone's guess but, knowing what he did, John could feel sorry for him. He spooned his coffee, tasted it, set it down.

'More sugar?' Mark reached for the bowl.

'Too hot,' John stared back through the window while his hands found and lit a cigarette. 'An interesting case, Yendle,' he said. 'A man with a grievance who has been used by regular enemy agents to do their dirty work for them. Even at that the thing is full of inconsistencies.'

'Such as?'

'Atom bombs aren't cheap, and they

aren't the easiest things to obtain. It was smuggled in, of course. A fast plane across the border and a dead-drop at a pick-up point would have taken care of that. Metal isn't hurt by impact with the ground, and the units could have been delivered separately.' John picked up his cup. 'What puzzles me is why use Yendle at all? Why not a regular agent?'

'Maybe they're running out of agents?' suggested Mark. 'Security rounded up most enemy nationals and the few that are left are under constant supervision. Perhaps they had to use one of our people in order to avoid suspicion?'

'Or as a guinea pig?' John swallowed his coffee, set down the cup, and refilled it from the pot. 'Suppose that they wanted to test our efficiency and, at the same time, remain safe. They could have used Yendle as a test-piece. The tip-off to the agent who reported him could have been fixed as could the radioactivity on his skin and clothing. Hypnotic conditioning would have tailored Yendle to almost anything they wanted.'

'I don't get it,' said Mark. 'If they used

him as a guinea pig, then that means that there needn't be a bomb at all.' He looked startled. 'Is it possible?'

'I think so.'

'But why? What would be the point in it?'

'Sabotage needn't stop at the destruction of material; it can be quite as effective in other ways. Ever since Yendle was arrested, thirteen hours ago now, every resource of Security has been channelled to track down the supposed bomb. But what if there is no bomb? What then?'

'No harm has been done,' said Mark promptly.

'This time, no, but what of the future?' John looked pensive. 'You've heard of the story of the boy who cried 'Wolf.' In the end no one believed him when the wolves really came. Suppose that we have a series of such incidents, we can guess what would happen. Security would get rattled, and, in order to protect the country, would bear down even harder than at present. People would grumble, protest and the pressure would increase. In the end we would become a total totalitarian state, ruled by Security under the justification of guarding against sabotage. Incidentally, we are not so far from that unhappy state of affairs at the present.'

'I can't agree with you,' said Mark shortly. 'We are a democratic people who have yielded some of our personal liberty in order to fight a war. No loyal citizen can protest against the regulations designed to protect his country.'

'And if he does, of course, then he isn't loyal.' John didn't press the point. 'There is another possibility if it turns out that there is no bomb. Continued scares and threats which turn out negative may have the effect of lulling people into a false sense of security. Then, when no one really believes in the threats . . . ' He made a motion with his hands.

'It's logical,' admitted Mark slowly. He stared down at the cup in his hand.

'It's more than logical,' said John. 'It's pure psychological engineering.'

'Do you believe that this is the case? That there is no bomb?'

'Not really. Any such plan as I have

described requires a long-term policy and a shrewd understanding of our national character. Also, again taking the long-term view there is little point in one totalitarian state forcing another of a different system to adopt their regime. It would be the same as making your opponent as fit and as strong as yourself. They firmly believe that our strength, our democracy, is our weakness. The trouble is that we are wasting our strength to become something which we profess to despise. Security, while ideal on paper, cannot be enforced without adopting some of the attributes of a totalitarian regime.'

'That, of course, is your personal opinion?' Mark seemed a little strained.

'That is more psychological engineering,' said John. 'And, as a psychologist, you should know it as well as I do. Once people stop becoming men and women and start becoming units, then we have hit the skids away from democracy. It is too easy to be impersonal about a unit, too easy to justify actions that hurt some but are for the supposed good of many.

Society is not an entity, but a collection of individuals. True democracy dies the moment we ignore that fact.'

'Perhaps.' Mark didn't want to talk about it. Privately, he considered Evans to be a doddering old fool, whose tongue would get him into trouble if he didn't watch it. As a psychologist he was good, Mark had to admit that, but even an expert psychologist couldn't hope to retain his high Security rating if he went around talking such subversive nonsense. He changed the subject.

'What are we going to do about Yendle?'

'Crack him, naturally; there is nothing else we can do.' John stared through the window at the slumped figure on the uncomfortable chair. 'Get me a pistol, some bullets, and ask Colonel Malcome to come here as soon as possible.'

The pistol was a .45 service model and the bullets seemed, to John, to be unnecessarily brutal. He imagined being shot with one, cringed at the imagined impact of lead against his flesh, then demanded to be shown how the gun was

loaded, how it worked and other important details.

'When did the colonel say he would be
here?'

'Soon.' Mark was curious. 'He has
some work to clear up before he can leave
the office. Why did you want the gun?'

'Psychology uses many weapons,' said
John mildly. 'Drugs, hypnosis, shock therapy,
induced insanity, even outright surgery. It
can even use force.' He toyed with the
pistol, loading the magazine, working the
slide and watching the cartridge slip into
the breech. He unloaded the pistol, expelled
the cartridges from the magazine and began
to fill it again. 'How do you . . . ?' He
grunted. 'Never mind, I can see how it
works.'

'Be careful,' warned Mark. 'That thing
can kill people.' He glanced through the
window, then at John, his eyes incredulous. 'Yendle?'

'Yendle is in a peculiar mental state,'
said John. He fumbled with the gun,
nodded, and expelled all the cartridges
again. They lay on the desk before him,
gleaming copper and brass in the brilliant

lighting. He rested the gun beside them, the dark metal and plastic grip holding the beauty of a well-designed mechanism.

The door opened and Malcome walked into the office.

He glanced at the gun, stared through the window, and sat down. 'Well?'

'We were talking of Yendle,' said John softly. 'He is in a peculiar mental state at the moment. When he was arrested he immediately went into near-hysteria. It was artificially induced, but quite effective. He rode the crest of one end of his emotional cycle and felt literally on top of the world. While in that state nothing could touch him, but there was one thing wrong with it, it couldn't last.'

'So?'

'So Yendle is now on his way down to the other end of his emotional cycle, the manic depressive stage. From feeling wonderful he will feel, literally, like hell. He will be tormented by guilt and fear and utter depression, and death, to him, will be an escape from an unendurable existence. The condition will be exaggerated, of course. A normal man does not normally swing to the extremes of his emotional cycle in twenty-four hours. We can thank his friends for that, the ones who planted all the hypnotic conditioning, but, artificial or not, it will be just as effective. Unless he is executed he will commit suicide.'

John picked up the gun and toyed with it. Malcome glanced at it, looked surprised, then concentrated on what John was saying.

'But don't imagine, even then, that you will learn anything from him. He will remain silent because any information he gives may serve to alleviate his punishment, and that will be the last thing he desires.'

'Then there is no hope?' Malcome glanced again at the pistol John was holding. The doctor was now toying with the bullets, lifting each one and slipping it into the magazine. 'What's that thing for?'

'There is another aspect to the problem,' said John. He ignored the question. 'Yendle will give us the information we want only when he wants to give it. We cannot take it from him against his will, and he knows it. He also knows that, once we have it, his protection will be gone. The trick, obviously, is to make him want to give it to us.'

'You make it sound easy,' said Malcome. He stared through the window at the slumped figure on the uncomfortable chair. 'Damn the swine! Making us sit here and wait for the blow-up. When I think of all those people . . . ' His big hands knotted.

'You'd like to kill him, wouldn't you?' said John softly. The click of the magazine as he thrust it into the pistol punctuated his words. 'You'd like to beat him to a pulp with your bare hands. You'd like to take a gun and lift it to his head and watch his face as he screams and begs for mercy, the mercy he is denying to all those decent men and women who are going to die unless he talks. You'd like to kill him because he has beaten you, because he has laughed at you and what you stand for. You'd like to kill him because he is a dirty traitor and not fit to be alive.'

He stared into the frosty blue eyes, operated the slide of the pistol, and put the weapon into the colonel's hand.

'Kill him, Malcome. He's no good to us now. Kill him and rid the earth of a little of its vermin. Kill him before he can do any more damage. Kill him . . . kill him . . . '

His voice droned on.

* * *

Yendle sat on his chair, his face between his hands, and felt misery tear at his soul. The discomfort of the chair didn't bother him; if anything he welcomed it. He was, though he couldn't know it, in much the same state of mind as an old-time penitent. Pain, physical pain, was welcome to him. Confession would have been an even greater relief, but that was the one thing he could not do.

His survival instinct, as yet, was still too strong.

His hate was even stronger. He hated the people who had done this to him, not his friends, but the uniformed fools who had ruled and ruined his life ever since he was a boy. He was glad that he had them worried; gladder still that they would suffer. He only wished that he could kill them all and so rid the earth of the strutting, egotistical, self-opinionated swine.

He gritted his teeth as he thought about them. Let them hurt him! Let them kill him, even; not that they would. He was safe as long as they didn't know where the bomb was hidden, and they wouldn't know about that until it blew. For some reason he never thought about what would happen after that.

The hate did not last. No emotion could last in his present state, for hate, like love, fought a losing battle against his overpowering depression. He slumped even more on the chair, great waves of self-pity engulfing him like the black tides of the limitless ocean.

It had been a rotten life. Nothing he had done had met with success. He had been dogged every step of the way by Security, and all because of a couple of mistakes which hadn't even been his fault. It wasn't fair that a man should have to suffer from something he had done in the past. It wasn't right that a thing, done when legal, should be considered illegal after the lapse of years. It wasn't just, and it wasn't decent. And the worst part of it was that no one agreed with him.

Aside from others like him, of course, they knew, they had been through the same mill. They could understand how it was that a man wanted to hit back at the thing that damned him. They felt the same way. It was only justice to cause trouble in return for trouble received. It was the only way a man could get even, when the courts and the police and everyone jumped on him just because he had a bad name. And he hadn't committed a single crime, not one. He would have been better treated had he been a murderer.

He didn't raise his head at the click of the door. He felt too listless to rise to his feet, to follow the uniformed fool into the next room to be asked more endless questions. To hell with him! To hell with everyone. Why didn't they leave him alone?

'Yendle!' The voice was as cold as fate. 'Yendle, you dirty swine!'

A hand gripped the hair at the back of his head, jerked, and he stared into a granite face with frosty eyes and a crease for a mouth.

'I'm going to kill you, Yendle!'

A hand swung upwards, a hand weighted with the black bulk of a pistol. The weapon steadied and Yendle stared directly into the muzzle.

Malcome pulled the trigger.

★　★　★

'It worked!' Malcome sat in the office with John and Mark, and sounded as if even now he couldn't believe it. 'They found the bomb with thirty minutes to spare. It was atomic, all right, a hand-made outfit disguised as a recorder.' He became grim. 'Hand-made or not, it would have wiped out Alamushta, the factory and half the inhabitants. The fall-out would have taken care of the other half and about five square miles of territory.'

'Did you find out why there was a time-lag?'

'It was set to go off at change of shift and just when a consignment of raw materials coincided with a delivery of finished products.' Malcome didn't say what the products were, but John could guess. Alamushta was a new town, one that had sprung up to serve a factory that had been built shortly after the establishment of the first base on the Moon. It wasn't hard to put two and two together to come out with the obvious four.

'You took a gamble,' said Malcome. 'If Yendle hadn't cracked . . . '

'He had to crack.'

'But you couldn't be sure,' insisted Malcome. 'I still say that you took a chance.'

'What had we to lose?' John sighed as he stared through the window into the empty cell. Yendle had long since been carried away, curled up with his knees touching his chin in the foetal position of dementia praecox. 'But it wasn't the risk it seemed. We had all the advantage. Yendle was a national, he was in the transition stage between hysteria and manic depressive, and you sincerely wanted to kill him.' He smiled at the colonel. 'Incidentally, I must apologize for having hypnotized you.'

'Did you?' Malcome looked startled. 'I didn't know that.'

'It was the only way to get you to go into that cell with the fixed determination to kill.' John turned as Mark went to the door and returned with coffee. 'It wasn't hard to convince you. You had been working for long hours at high concentration. You had had your hatred of Yendle and what he stood for sharpened to a fine edge. It was a simple thing to get you to the killing stage, and even simpler to get you to go into the cell. All you did was to do what you wanted to do. All I did was to nullify your censor just enough to permit you to do it.'

'I forgive you,' said Malcome. He accepted a cup from Mark, stirred it, sipped, helped himself to more sugar. 'Yendle talked, anyway.'

'Yes,' said John soberly. 'He talked.' He didn't like to remember the frenzied rush of words and the ghastly collapse. He didn't even like to remember the expression on the colonel's face when he had gone in to kill. Yendle had cracked simply because there was nothing else for him to do, but he had paid for it by a desperate retreat into the past.

'The key was survival,' he explained. 'With an enemy national it would have been different; his personal survival instinct would have yielded to that of his people and country. You could have torn such a man apart before he would have broken. You yourself would be the same. You would make any personal sacrifice for your country because, to you, the survival of your nation is far more important than merely saving your own life. Yendle wasn't like that.'

'He was a traitor,' said Malcome.

'He was a man without loyalty,' corrected John. 'The enemy meant nothing to him and he had no patriotism. He was an individual and, because of that, his own survival was of paramount

66

importance.' John shrugged. 'I am speaking, of course, of the time when you went in to him.'

'Couldn't we have used that technique earlier?' Mark leaned forward, his round, Nordic face intent as he listened to the doctor.

'No.'

'Why not?' Malcome handed John his coffee. 'Here, it's getting cold.'

'Thanks.' John took it, tasted it, drank it down. He fumbled for a cigarette, found only an empty package, and looked wistfully inside.

'Here.' Malcome passed over a fresh pack. 'Keep them.'

'Thanks.' John ripped open the pack, shook out a cigarette, lit it, inhaled with grateful pleasure. 'We had to wait until Yendle's hysteria had died and he had begun the swing towards the manic depressive stage. We had to wait until the time was just right for the attack on his survival instinct. Too early and he would have laughed at it; too late and he would have craved for death as an escape from misery. We had to hit him when he was 'normal.' So you took a gun and went in to kill him. He knew you intended to kill him, because you did intend to kill him. You weren't acting, you were going to lift that gun to his head and blow his brains out.' John drew at his cigarette and stared thoughtfully through the smoke.

'Sincerity is something which cannot be counterfeited. His subconscious recognized your intent and he broke. His survival instinct took over and saved him in the only way possible. But had that gun been loaded, as you thought it was, he would have died before the words could leave his mouth.'

'I doubt it,' said Malcome. 'I gave him plenty of time.'

'You gave him no time at all,' corrected John. 'Both Mark and myself saw you press the trigger. If I hadn't fixed the magazine so that a cartridge couldn't enter the chamber Yendle would have died. It would have been a kindness at that.'

'I don't remember it.' Malcome frowned. 'I knew the gun was loaded, of course. I saw you load it. But that would have provided the best reason of all for me not to fire. I wanted information, not an execution.'

'You wanted a dead traitor,' said John. 'You wanted it so much that it was easy to persuade you to go into that cell with the intent to kill. It was because of that intent that Yendle broke. You provided no alternative.'

'So I would have killed him,' Malcome admitted. 'All that proves is that I hate traitors.'

'Yes,' said John softly. 'But is it normal for a man to hate the very thing he has helped to create?'

The silence was the calm before the storm.

★   ★   ★

Malcome was a colonel attached to Security, a man who had devoted his life to the furtherance of secrecy and the stamping out of disloyalty. His reactions were both violent and immediate. John heard him out, mentally checking his protests against a list of possible reactions. He was pleased to find that he hadn't missed one.

'Finished?' He lit a fresh cigarette. 'Now let's be sensible about this. I am not accusing you, personally, of anything. What you stand for is something else again. Surely, you have noticed that the tighter Security clamps down the higher the sabotage rate mounts? Little things mostly, petty, infuriating little things which, on the surface, seem without rhyme or reason. I am talking of sabotage now, colonel, not treason.'

'Anything which hampers our efficiency helps the enemy,' said Malcome coldly. 'Anything which helps the enemy is an act of treason.'

'Therefore, anyone performing an act of sabotage must, by your logic, be working for the enemy.' John shrugged. 'Any schoolboy could tell you the illogic of such a syllogism. Your conclusion just isn't true.'

'A traitor is a traitor,' said Mark. 'You can't get away from that.'

'I am speaking of saboteurs, not traitors, captain.'

'They are the same.'

'They are not the same. A traitor is, by definition, someone who betrays his country or friends or cause. Sabotage is damage done with deliberate intent. The mechanic who tends your car and, at the same time, damages it so as to make business, is guilty of sabotage. Even you would hardly accuse him of treason. Yendle was not a traitor.'

'Sophistry,' sneered Malcome. 'Perhaps we should have given the swine a medal for planting that bomb.'

'It would be better if we tried to find out why he wanted to plant it in the first place.' John slapped the dossier before him. 'The reason is in here. Yendle was hounded all his life by Security for being a suspected subversive. There was nothing against him but the fact that he had once donated some money to an authorised fund, had read a book later proscribed, and had tangled with a long-hair movement for world peace. We did the hounding, colonel. We are to blame for what Yendle became.'

'There can be no possible excuse for a

man becoming a traitor,' said the colonel stiffly.

'I disagree. A man can only be loyal to something he believes in and, if his loyalty has been crushed, then how can he be accused of disloyalty? What cause did Yendle have? What interest, other than the accident of birth, did he have in this country? He was treated worse than any criminal for actions which, in themselves, were harmless. Is it any wonder that he wanted to hit back?'

'You are tired, doctor,' said Mark hastily. 'You've been up all night and have been working under a great strain. You'll feel better after a good rest.'

'Yes,' said John dully. 'I'll feel better, but nothing can alter the facts. We are a democracy founded by a freedom-loving people who, remember this, gained their freedom by revolt against authority. We are still called a free people. We permit freedom of speech — on paper — and then penalise a man for using it. We claim religious and political tolerance — and you know how empty that boast is. We tell our people that they are adult — and then force them to wear blinkers for fear that they should know too much. We claim internal equality for all peoples — and have lived with that lie for a hundred and fifty years.'

'We are a free people,' said Malcome. 'But we are at war, and in time of war the individual has to relinquish some of his rights for the common good. Security has to be hard. Better a few people should suffer a little inconvenience than run the risk of men like Yendle destroying us.'

'A little inconvenience?' John smiled but his eyes did not smile. He was treading on dangerous ground and he knew it. It was better to shut his mouth, to let things ride, to ignore the facts which his training had found in all the reports and investigations, the mounting suspicions that all was not as it should be. Psychological engineering was a thing understood by few, and certainly not by the military. But a man had to try.

'You hounded Yendle all his life,' he said. 'He was on your lists as a suspected subversive, and yet that did not prevent him from planting the bomb. The only possible justification for such persecution was to prevent what actually happened. Maybe if we had trusted him a little more, given him a stake in the country he lived in and was supposed to live for, he wouldn't have wanted to do it. You can't treat a man like a dog and expect him not to resent it. Not when our history and culture rest on the belief that every man is as good as his neighbour. We gained our freedom by a revolt against authority once, remember. The same spirit is alive today.'

'Rebellion?' Malcome was genuinely shocked. 'Impossible!'

'Nothing is impossible, colonel,' reminded John tiredly. 'Only highly improbable.'

'It's an interesting theory,' said Mark. He reached towards the tray. 'Have some more coffee, doctor. Black isn't it?'

'With plenty of sugar.' John smiled, grateful for the help the captain was offering, but he knew that it could do no good. He had gone too far, said too much, and Malcome would not forget. But it wouldn't hurt to keep up the pretence.

'The rebellion has already started,' he said quietly. 'Small rebellions, but all the more annoying because of that. The saboteurs who, without really knowing what they do, or why they do it, are causing so much trouble. They aren't traitors, colonel, though we execute them as such. If there was a real, fighting war, they would be the first to volunteer. I like to think of them as patriots fighting for a lost cause. They are fighting for freedom.'

'Nonsense.' Malcome seemed about to say more but thought better of it. 'If it wasn't for Security, this nation would be overrun with enemy agents and our freedom lost.' He snorted. 'Anyway, even allowing the possibility of your . . . theory, what could we do about it? To be effective Security must be stringent. We simply cannot afford to take chances, and the only way to achieve that is the system we use.'

'It is small consolation for a man to be thrown into jail because of the possibility that the man in the next cell might, one day, commit a crime,' said John.

'Perhaps.' Malcome wasn't interested.

He glanced at his wrist, gulped his coffee and rose to his feet. 'It's getting late, almost dawn. Will you be sleeping here, doctor?'

'No, thank you, not if I can catch a plane back.'

'There's one at dawn,' said Mark. He yawned and rubbed his eyes. 'I'll be glad to get some rest. We've all been under a terrific strain, and the sight of Yendle after his collapse wasn't very nice.' He yawned again. 'Funny how your mind works when you're tired. I remember one time, just before some examinations it was, that I dreamed up an entire scheme to gain control of the world.' He laughed, self-consciously. 'It was just one of those weird ideas you get.'

'Like saboteurs being patriots?' said Malcome. He smiled. 'I understand.' He held out his hand to the doctor.

'Thank you for all you've done,' he said sincerely. 'I don't have to tell you how grateful we all are. If it hadn't been for you an entire town would now be radioactive ash.' He chuckled. 'Think of that the next time you grow tired, doctor.

It may serve to show how fragile your theories are.'

'He won't report it,' said Mark, after the colonel had gone. 'But, man, do you take risks!'

He wasn't joking.

* * *

The plane didn't leave at dawn. An inspector had discovered a couple of cut wires and the skyline was grounded for two hours for inspection and repairs. John spent the time reading, thinking, and wondering how it was all going to end.

Moving a mountain was hardly a job for one man, but sometimes he had to try.

Even though he could only get hurt.

2

The Devil's Dictionary

I saw the book on the second-hand counter of Manlick's bookstore. It was tucked away among a lot of popular trash and the bound files of out-of-date magazines. At first I thought that it was a bible, one of the thick, leather-bound affairs which used to be popular years ago when they were used more as a family record than as a book of comfort and guidance. Then I picked it up and riffled the pages and immediately knew that I had found what I had been looking for.

Not the book itself, of course, but any book that was a bargain. You don't get many of them nowadays, though the odd item is still to be picked up from where it is hidden among rubbish. Most booksellers check their stock pretty thoroughly so that there are slim pickings for the expert to find. I am an expert in a small way, at least I can tell the first editions from the reprinted copies, the rare works from those which look good but are valueless, and I can date a book as well as the next man.

The book I was holding was old.

The paper was the thick, heavy, hand-made kind you just don't get now. The lettering was the black-text style with the cursives and flourishes that Caxton first introduced when he set up shop from the continent. The text was, of course, in Latin, and several pages had been hand-illuminated with gold leaf and colourful pigments.

I can read a little Latin and what I read made me all the more determined to purchase the volume. Manlick was watching me — it doesn't take long for a bookseller to classify his customers — and his little eyes narrowed as I showed him the book.

'How much for the relic?'

'Relic?' He took it, flipped the pages, and pretended to know more than he did. 'Where did you find it?'

'Down with the junk.' I took the book

from his hands and opened the front cover. 'No price marked.'

'Ten pounds?'

We argued, of course, but he didn't really know what the book was worth and I knew he couldn't read Latin.

We settled for five pounds after I had shown him the scarred binding and the mildewed pages and lied about how much it would cost to restore the book to a decent condition. After the sale he relaxed a little and I asked him from where the book had come.

'It's part of a library I bought from Sir Clement's estate.' He shrugged. 'You know how these libraries are. Plenty of Victorian stuff, some good first editions, a mess of rubbish and one or two really good items. That book must have been among the rubbish. I had Winslow sort the stuff out for me and he's a good man.'

He was, too good, and I wondered just how he had let this item slip past his shrewd evaluation of the worth of any book ever printed. I didn't let it worry me, finding old books is similar to a treasure hunt, quite often the regular search is a waste of time but occasionally the rewards are high.

Back home I unwrapped my prize and gave it a closer examination.

Dating it was hard because there was neither printer's imprint or date of publication but I placed it as mid-seventeenth century. I had been right about the hand-illumination, someone had illustrated the book with gold-leaf and pigments and, looking at it, I was reminded of the old manuscripts of the past. That dated it still further because the tendency after printing first became introduced was to copy the old manuscripts as far as possible.

If it hadn't been for the faint impression of the type on the reverse side of the paper, the elaborate cursives and gothic text, I'd have thought that the entire missal had been hand-produced.

I managed to read two pages, struggling with the Latin and frowning over the blurred type. Two pages were enough. I had read just enough to know that what I had found was no ordinary book of prayer or sermons. There was something vaguely disquieting in the hints contained in the introduction but my knowledge of the dead language wasn't good enough for me to do more than gain a hint at what the book contained.

I decided to take it to Henshaw.

George Henshaw was a recluse who had bound himself with books and dead knowledge. I had met him one day while making some researches at the British Museum and, from a casual nodding acquaintanceship, we had become as close as two people of naturally reserved natures could be. He lived on the top floor of an old rambling house bequeathed to him by a dead aunt, one of those horrible Georgian style houses still to be seen in some parts of the city, and the lower part of the house was filled with the most indescribable collection of curios I have ever seen outside of a museum.

I had heard whispers about George from those who should have known what they were talking about. As a young man he had travelled the world and spent much time in Tibet. Back in London he had become involved with a cult of

Satanists and, for a time, had lived on the thin edge of the law. There had been a nasty exposé concerning the death of a young man at a ceremony and George, disgusted with the aims and objects of the cult, had withdrawn from all association with them.

That didn't concern me. What did interest me was that George had an astounding knowledge of Latin and his collection of old books of a specific nature was unequalled by any man or institution in the country. If anyone could tell me just what it was that I had found it would be he.

'It's old,' he admitted after I had shown him my prize. 'Where did you say it came from?'

'Sir Clement's library. Manlick must have bought the lot cheap and had Winslow check them for him. How Winslow ever came to overlook this I shall never know.' I smiled as I touched the old, cracked leather of the binding. 'Lucky for me he did, though.'

'Winslow is a religious man,' he said absently. 'I'm only surprised that he didn't destroy the book.' He stared at me, his thin face serious in the fading light of day. I smiled at his expression.

'Burn it? Why should he have done? And what has his being a religious man to do with it?'

'There is some knowledge better lost,' George said quietly. 'Not because, in itself, it is bad, but for the misuse which may be made of it by others. This book,' again he rested his hand on the scarred cover, 'contains such knowledge.'

'Please.' I was a little annoyed at my friend and impatient to discover the book's true worth. A staunch materialist, I had little patience with those who hinted at mysterious knowledge and hidden secrets. Such tales were, for me, the vapid outpourings of diseased minds. I picked up the book and opened it at the introduction.

'Let's get down to it. From what I can make out it was written by a monk, and printed in the mid-seventeenth century. Now, there is something odd right away. The monasteries were dissolved by then and few if any books were produced by monks at that time. Certainly they weren't printed.' I looked at George. 'I'd say that this volume is a copy of an earlier work. Would you agree?'

He didn't answer straight away but, taking the book, switched on a desk lamp and held the open page in the cone of brilliance. For a long time he read the awkward text, his lips moving silently as he followed the Latin, then he looked up at me with an expression that contained both anticipation and surprise.

'You are right,' he said. 'The original was written late in the twelfth century by a monk of the Franciscan Order, a Brother Shwartz of Berthanbolm, in a monastery buried deep in the Hartz mountains. The introduction gives his history and makes it quite plain that the Brother was burned for heresy and dabbling in the black arts.' George leaned back in his chair, his thin hands resting on the book, his eyes behind their thick lenses serious.

'In short, John, you have found a copy of an authentic Grimoire, a handbook for witches and wizards.'

'Is that all?' I was disappointed. Grimoires, while of interest to those concerned with old fables and magic spells, had only a limited market. I had hoped that the book would prove to be of more general interest. I held out my hand for the volume but George was reading on and seemed not to have noticed my gesture. So deep was his concentration that I left him and busied myself with studying some of his collection. I had seen his books before but now, for the first time, I noticed that, masked by harmless-looking covers, many of them were similar works to the one I had found. Grimoires of Black and White magic, books of spells and incantations, many of them with intricate diagrams and long lists of formula for magic potions. I was reading a recipe for the making of a Glory Hand, the dismembered hand of a corpse treated in a special way and which was said to have the power of opening all locks, when a sudden exclamation from my friend caused me to close the book and stare at him.

'What is it, George?'

'This is wonderful!' There could be no mistaking his enthusiasm. 'John! Do you realise what you have found?'

'An old book on Black Magic,' I said. 'Why?'

'This is one of the genuine volumes which escaped the great burning of the dark ages.' George was really excited. 'The text explains just how it came to be in print. It seems that a small group of practitioners, persecuted and hounded by the Church and the civil authorities, disbanded their libraries and buried most of their works. Some of them, however, tried a second way to preserve the forbidden knowledge. They chose to do it by multiple records. They bribed a printer to produce a thousand copies of the book and intended to spread them among the initiated over the then-known world. It was a good plan and might well have succeeded but for the faint-heartedness of the printer. He informed the authorities and the entire stock of books, together with the original manuscript and the galley-proofs, were destroyed. This book, obviously a proof to be checked against the final production, is the only one to have survived. Naturally, the illuminations and binding were added later.'

'So we have the rarest of First Editions,' I said interestedly. 'One single copy of one single print-order. It should be worth quite a sum.'

'It is,' he said, and hesitated. 'How much were you thinking of asking, John?'

It was my turn to hesitate. If the book was as rare as he said then I could ask my own price from those collectors interested in such things. It might even be worth my while to offer it to the British Museum or to the institutions abroad. Against this was my friendship with George who obviously wanted the volume for himself. I tried to find a middle way.

'I don't want to rob you, George, but at the same time, not having a private income as you have, I want to make as much as I can.'

'I'll give you twenty thousand pounds,' he said curtly. 'Well?'

Again I hesitated. Twenty thousand pounds was, to me, a lot of money.

'How about if I had it photocopied,

George? You would then have an authentic copy and it wouldn't cost you anywhere near as much?'

'No.' He smiled at me and I recognised the light of the collector gleaming in his eyes. I had seen it before and knew that, no matter how much I asked, he would do his best to raise the sum. 'Thank you, John, but no. It wouldn't be the same. Twenty-five thousand and that's my top figure.'

'I'll take the twenty thousand,' I said. 'If you want it that badly I can't refuse you.'

He smiled and wrote me out a cheque without hesitation and, after I had folded it and put it in my pocket, he picked up the book again as though he couldn't bear to be parted from it.

'I suppose you think I'm a little insane, John,' he said quietly. 'Maybe I am, but to me this book is worth all I own.'

'As a collector's item?' I smiled and shook my head. 'It can be an expensive hobby, George.'

'Yes and no,' he said seriously. 'I know you, John, and know that you are a strict materialist. You don't believe in this sort of thing, do you?'

'Black Magic?' I shook my head. 'Childish superstitions born in ignorance and fed by the unthinking faith of the illiterate.'

'And the Alchemists?'

'Bunglers.' I smiled at his expression. 'Oh, I know that they are supposed to have been the early chemists and that, in their way, they tried to make honest discoveries. But the few things they did discover, gunpowder for example, were due to accident. They filled their experiments with verbal rubbish and appeals to non-existent spirits and demons. But what did they really do to help modern knowledge?'

'There are two ways of attacking any problem,' he said quietly. 'Much of the old science is, as you say, rubbish, but not all.' He relaxed in his chair and stared at me through his thick glasses.

'Sorcery in the Middle Ages was highly questionable. The average egoist was an outright charlatan. Some wizards hung around the courts of small nobles or petty princes, dabbling in astrology, palmistry and a little alchemy. They were totally ungenuine. Others were like modern confidence tricksters, forever asking for money to perfect their experiments in order to find the Elixir of Youth or the Philosopher's Stone with which to transmute base metals into gold. A third class were quack doctors, men who ran little shops in side streets and sold false love philters and who promised to put curses and spells on enemies. They, like the others, were also dishonest in that they could not do as they claimed.

'Mixed in with these impostors were the psychopathic cases. Demoniacs and diaboleptics who pranced naked on the hilltops during Walpurgis Eve and who claimed to be in communication with the Devil. There we have the clear evidence of inverted religious mania. Remember the Dancing Hysteria which swept over Europe at the time of the Crusades? But always there were serious students of the mantic arts. From their records, hidden as they are with allusion and symbolism, we, those of us who are interested, are trying to rediscover just what it was they knew.'

'But did they really know anything?' I admitted his sincerity but could not feel it myself. George nodded.

'Yes.' He smiled at my expression. 'Don't take my word for it. Science now recognises the pathological existence of the werewolf and vampire in mental cases. Science now recognises many practises today that once were labelled as witchcraft. The search for the Philosopher's Stone is one. We now transmute mercury into gold by the medium of the cyclotron. In the old days they also thought that they could change mercury into gold, but they tried it with heat and spells and incantations.'

'That's different,' I said quickly. 'That's science.'

'What is science but the search for the truth?' he said evenly. 'No, John, you can't damn all those old seekers after knowledge because they tried a different method than ourselves. True, they used to brew a mixture containing toads and foxgloves for heart troubles. Now we know that both toads and foxgloves contain digitalis — used now for the treatment of heart disease.'

He rose and crossed to his shelf of old volumes.

'Collected here, John, are the fruits of those early seekers after knowledge. A lot of it is rubbish, that I grant, still more is hopelessly shrouded in allusion and symbolism, but there was a good reason for that. Remember the times in which they were written, John. There was no tolerance then. Heresy earned death at the stake and anyone not following the strict line laid down by the Church was deemed a heretic. They had to be vague for their own protection. But I believe that they stumbled on things since lost to us. For hundreds of years men tried to find a path to knowledge and power. Riddled with superstition as they were, yet is it asking too much to believe that they may have learned something from all their experiments? That is what I hope to prove and, now that I have your book, there is no need for further delay.'

'So the book was important then?'

Almost I regretted selling it. George nodded.

'Yes. The writer of that book had done a tremendous amount of research and had correlated his findings in what we would call now, a scientific way. In effect it is what we would call a dictionary of scientific terms. The ancients had their terminology, you know, and not all of it meant what it appears to mean. With the book as a guide I am sure that we can conduct certain experiments with a fair degree of success.'

He meant it. He believed that he spoke nothing but the simple truth and, as I stared at him, I felt the first stirrings of excitement. I forced myself to appear calm.

'Do you actually mean to tell me that you think you can conjure up demons and spirits from the netherworld?'

'Did I say that?' He shrugged with the impatience of a man who has long been accustomed to misunderstanding. 'Let me repeat: the ancients tried a different path to knowledge. Where we depend on a frontal attack, force if you like, they tried to obtain their results by appealing or demanding aid from either the matter itself or from other-world entities. Don't scoff, John. If you had seen what I have seen . . . '

He broke off and I remembered his dabblings in the occult. I smiled and reached for my hat.

'Very well, George, I won't scoff, but one thing I'd like you to promise. When you get ready to conduct your experiments I'd like to be in on them. Agreed?'

He hesitated, then nodded. 'Agreed.'

I left him busy reading the old volume I had just sold him for twenty thousand pounds.

It was a month before I heard from George again. I heard of him from mutual acquaintances and one day I bumped into Fred Brown, an old bibliophile who knew as much about books as I did and whose collection of first editions was the envy of most of his friends. We had a drink together and over a small table in a secluded booth, he mentioned George.

'What's he up to?' Fred grinned at me

though his eyes were sharp. 'I've heard that he's getting mixed up with some of his old friends again. Frank tells me that he was in the old apothecary's, you know that herbalist's in Market Street, when he saw George collect an order. Dragon's Blood, powdered Mandrake, dried Mummy and dessicated toads as well as a lot of other stuff. Is George up to his Devil Worship again?'

'Not as far as I know.' I dismissed the incident with a shrug. 'From what I heard he wants to try some old recipes he found in an old Grimoire.'

'Black Magic!' Fred shuddered. 'The fool! He doesn't know what he's letting himself in for.'

'Do you?' I'd heard rumours about Fred and, though I liked the man, yet there was something reptilian about him. He grunted.

'Maybe I do and maybe I don't, that's neither here nor there. But if you're a friend of his you'll do your best to stop him messing about with powers he can't control or understand. Remember Sam Young?'

I blinked at the sudden change of subject.

'Why?'

'Never mind, why? Do you remember him or not?'

'Yes, I remember him.' I did too. Sam Young had been an artist of the modern school. That is, he starved while bewailing the fates that prevented his genius from being acknowledged. Now that Fred mentioned it I hadn't seen Sam for more than two years. I said as much.

'I'm not surprised,' said Fred grimly. 'He's kept locked up now and has been ever since his breakdown. Went stark, staring mad one night and tried to kill his landlady. They caught him in time, certified him, and put him away where he couldn't do any harm.' He leaned closer to me and lowered his voice. 'Sam tried messing about with old recipes. They say he was smeared all over with some kind of cream when they caught him. Why, I don't know, but he was seen shopping for much the same ingredients as your friend just before his breakdown.' He winked at me. 'A word to the wise . . . '

I nodded and sat for a long time over my drink after Fred had left. I hadn't given it much thought up till now. George's money had made life very easy for me and I had been busy tasting a little of the luxury I had always wanted but had never been able to afford. Now, because of what Fred had said, I began to feel a certain responsibility towards my friend and, leaving my drink unfinished on the table, I rose and headed for the British Museum. There were certain parchments that I wanted to consult as well as certain things I felt that I should obtain. Fred, despite his reputation, was a man I felt I could trust.

It was exactly five days later that George sent for me.

He was changed in a way I found hard to describe. He wasn't thinner than usual or gaunt or wasted. It was as if he had just awakened from sleep and was full of energy and enthusiasm. He met me at the door of his house and, as the portal closed behind me, thunder rippled over the darkened city and a brief flash of lightning illuminated his face through the transom. It died and the soft glow of candles replaced the electric fury. I looked at them.

'What's the matter with the lights, George?'

'They fused an hour ago.' He led me upstairs, talking all the time. 'Sorry to have sent for you so late, John, but I'm all ready to begin.' He chuckled, a sound of genuine anticipation and good humour. 'I suppose you're going to say why not wait until tomorrow, but why? I'm eager to get started and the sooner the better.' He opened the door and led the way into his study where, as I stripped off my overcoat, he sat down and poured out two glasses of wine.

'Thanks.' I sipped the wine and jumped as thunder shook the old house. 'A fine night for what you have in mind.'

'The thunder?' He shrugged. 'That isn't important. I doubt if the electrical content of the air will affect the formula in any serious way. The astrological predictions are just right, however. Mercury is in transit and Venus is in trine. The House of . . . '

'Please!' I held up my hand. 'You're talking Greek to me, I'm no astrologer. Is it important?'

'I don't know,' he admitted. 'It could be. I'm trying to think of the whole thing as a series of scientific experiments. The trouble is that we aren't too sure of what is important and what isn't. It is much like mixing a chemical formula, some things are indispensable, others can be added without real harm. Only, instead of measurable quantities of chemicals we are dealing with vibrations, angles, gases and combinations of intangibles any of which might be the key factor.'

He saw my expression and laughed.

'Don't look so bewildered, John. After all it was your book which provided the answer to my search.'

'But isn't it filled with the same fake gibberish as all the rest?'

'No.'

'Look,' I insisted. 'I've read some of that stuff and it usually doesn't make any sort of sense at all.'

'True, but there are kernels of truth and, never forget that most of it is illusion and symbolism. That is why the book you sold me is so important. It defines terms and quantities so as to make them understandable.' He sighed as he stared at me: 'Suppose, for example, you knew nothing of modern chemistry and found a formula for the making of gunpowder. It would read: Charcoal, fourteen per cent; sulphur, ten per cent; potassium nitrate, seventy-five per cent; water, one per cent. Understandable? To you now, perhaps, but how about to one of the old alchemists? He wouldn't know what 'per cent' meant and he would never have heard of potassium nitrate or sulphur. Convert the terms into his own terminology and you'd have something he could understand.'

'Charcoal, fourteen parts,' I said understandingly. 'Brimstone, ten parts; saltpetre, seventy-five parts and moisten with water.' I nodded.

'And the reverse applies,' George said impatiently. 'What did the old alchemists mean when they referred to 'The breath of the green dragon'? Some things we know are false, for example we know that any formula necessitating the powdered horn of Unicorn must mean something entirely different. Rhinoceros horn perhaps? Certainly not Unicorn, we know now that there is no such animal.' He glanced at his wristwatch and listened as thunder rolled overhead. 'No, John. Some of the spells are frauds; others are genuine.'

'You mean that if you read a spell aloud it would conjure up a demon?'

'If you read it correctly,' said George. 'That's the whole point and that is why we are here tonight, to find out the truth if possible within the framework of scientific experiment.' He tilted his head as a knock sounded from the door downstairs and, with a muttered apology, he left me to admit his guest.

I had never met Martin Lamas before and found him most interesting to look at. A thin, dried up little man with a head almost too big for his body and a trick of washing his hands as he spoke. His worn clothing revealed his poverty and, as he grinned and sipped at his wine, I was conscious of his eyes, small and sharp like those of a bird, flickering around the snug study as if in search of something.

'We were talking of reading spells,' said George. 'That is why I invited Martin to take a part in our experiment. You know, of course, that all the old incantations are written in Latin. You also know that, no one now knows just how the Latin was pronounced. We can read it, talk it, but we do not know how the original Romans sounded their syllables. It is as if an American were to read an English essay. It would sound recognisable but there would be stress placed on the wrong vowels and, as far as the vibrations went, it would sound totally different.' George leaned forward. 'The vibrations, John! That is the whole secret of the old incantations! The words themselves mean nothing, it is only the vibrations set up in pronouncing them which is important. That is why most of the spells read like ridiculous gibberish. Can you understand?'

'Yes,' I said, and I did. 'You are saying that the vibrations may act on the intangible plane separating us from the

Unknown in the same way as a certain tone may affect the sonic-lock of a door. We could set the lock of such a door to open only to a series of notes of music or vibrations of sound. Any words that gave the correct sounds would do. Any words — if spoken correctly. A lock set to the English phrase 'Pass the Tomato', would fail to open if an American spoke the words because he would use the short instead of the long 'a'.'

'Exactly.' George seemed pleased. 'Any words. Perhaps the well-known phrase 'Open Sesame' had some such original significance, but we wander from the point. Martin here, as far as anyone can tell, is the only man now capable of speaking Latin with the original pronunciation. At least, he says that he is, maybe we shall find out for sure tonight.'

Thunder rolled as the little man nodded and sipped at his wine. Unaccountably I shivered and, even as I did so, wondered why.

We sat and talked and drank wine until it was almost midnight and then George led us downstairs to the big, unused dining room of the old house. When I had last seen it, it had been filled with heavy, old-fashioned furniture, but now it was empty, with heavy drapes hanging from the ceiling and against the walls. Some equipment stood on the parquet floor and, on a table pushed against one wall, jars and boxes rested with sticks of chalk and rolled parchments.

'These are our ingredients,' said George. 'Corpse fat candles and phosphorescent chalk. Blood, I bought that from a man I know, and other things all of interest and, if I may say so, all very hard to obtain nowadays. Still,' he chuckled, 'it's surprising how easy it is to get the most out of things when it is possible to pay for them. And all genuine and guaranteed, even to the dried Mummy and powdered toadstools.' He drew a deep breath. 'Now, John, and you too Martin, let us be serious. This is in the nature of an experiment and we must approach it exactly as we would any other experiment. If we are successful we may open doors to knowledge undreamed of. Wealth, fame, power; if only a part of what the ancients believed comes true, then we shall have the world at our feet.'

Martin nodded and, even though I still felt the faint superciliousness of a man who knew quite well that all this was but make-believe, I too became serious. I became more than that. I became as acutely interested as George himself for, if by some incredible chance the experiment should work, then, as he had said, we should have control of powers unknown in the world today.

Intently I watched him prepare for the ritual.

On the smooth floor he traced a pentagram with the chalk, which glowed with an evil blue light of its own.

A small fire was lit in a brazier and candles, thick and odoriferous, set around the pentagram. Strange, cabalistic signs were traced with red and green and yellow pigments and a convoluted spiral writhed around the pentagram and symbols as if it were a serpent swallowing its own tail.

'The pentagram is the focus, as you might call it,' said George. 'I've made certain that it is mathematically correct and that the angles are as specified. The symbols also are said to have a restraining influence and the outer ring should bolster them so as to provide a measure of safety against anything which we may conjure up.' He moved around outside the circle and iron rubbed against the polished wood.

'Cold iron is also said to be a guard against demons,' said George. He dabbed at his face and I noticed that he was sweating. 'The incantation I have chosen for this experiment is Abbot Richalmus's spell to call up a draconibus. It is clearly laid out in his *Liber Revelationum de Insidia et Versutiis Daemonum Adversus Homines*. It is supposed to be a very effective spell and, now that we have the knowledge from the new Grimoire, I think that we can hope for success.'

'Wait a moment. I thought that you were going to call up the Devil,' I said. 'What's a draconibus?'

'A flying cacodemon of the night,' said George shortly. 'What made you think I intended to call up Satan?'

'Why not?' The fumes from the candles, or it may have been the wine, had made me a little light-headed. 'If we want power isn't he the one to give it to us?'

'Perhaps, but obviously you have forgotten what you have learned.' George was surprisingly abrupt. 'Satan never gives anything for nothing. If he gives you something be sure that it will cost you dear in the end.' He glanced at his wrist. 'Enough of talk. Are we ready?'

Martin nodded and picked up a scroll, one of several lying on the table. I nodded and stepped back against the wall, my hand in my pocket, my eyes watchful. George, after a last examination of the pentagram, scooped something from a box and crossed to a brazier.

And then everything began to grow unreal.

I saw him cast something on the flames and a flaring gout of colour rose towards the ceiling and painted the room with flickering shades of red and green and yellow. The fires died and thick, incense-like smoke welled from the brazier and dimmed the guttering light of the candles. Outside the thunder rolled as if to a fiendish accompaniment to the work inside the old house and, as it snarled about us, I saw Martin unroll his scroll and begin to read.

And then I became afraid.

I had never believed that human tongue could utter such sounds. The Latin, but a Latin I had never before heard, rolled from his throat in a jarring harmony of vibration and, as it swelled around us, I saw George, his face a perspiring mask, move swiftly about the room. He threw powders onto the brazier and smoke and colours blossomed beneath his hands. Liquid gurgled from a flask and my nostrils twitched to the scent of burning blood. He scattered perfume and strange spices into the pentagram and, all the time he worked, the little man's voice rose louder and louder until it seemed that all the city would be able to hear him above the noise of the storm.

And yet I knew that it was only a local illusion. It wasn't that Martin's voice had really risen louder but that the sounds he was uttering had taken on a peculiar penetrating quality. They acted as the screech of a nail against a slate or the droning sub-harmonics of a dentist's drill played on the nerves. It seemed to me that the power and tension within the room would soon burst beyond the walls and spill out into the street and, faintly behind me from the direction of the table, I heard the splinter of glass as a phial shattered beneath the ghastly vibrations which seemed almost able to tear soul from body.

The tension mounted, higher, higher, and then, with something like an unearthly scream, the little man threw back his head and, together with the snarling crack of thunder, shouted the last line of the hellish incantation set down by a man long dead.

Silence. A silence which was heavy with the coiling after-echoes of thundering vibrations and the subdued pulse of unimagined terrors. The air was thick with smoke and incense, nauseating with odours from the various powders George had flung into the brazier, and sickly with the scent of the corpse fat candles.

Silence — and that was all.

How long I stood there, my hand tight around the thing in my pocket, my lips pressed tightly together so that the muscles of my face ached from the strain I shall never know. I stared into the smoke and the haze and, it may have been imagination or it may have not, but it seemed to me as if something writhed in the smoke and moved so that the drifting clouds took on a squat and horribly human form. I blinked and shook myself as the curtains rattled back from the windows and the cold night air dispersed the smoke.

'We failed,' said George dully. 'The incantation didn't work.'

He snapped the light switch and cursed when no lights appeared. I, in order to get away from the fog, offered to repair the fuse and when I had done so rejoined them in the big room. In the harsh electric light the brazier and chalk marks on the floor seemed the foolish playthings of children and it was hard to believe that I had cringed with terror beneath the vibrations of a voice and the unseen, but tangible hint of an unearthly presence.

We talked about it over wine and biscuits in George's study.

'It must have been the thunder,' said George. 'Did you notice how it drowned out the sound of Martin's voice here? At times I could hardly hear what he was saying. The thunder must have disrupted the vibrational pattern just enough to render the incantation useless.' He seemed to cheer up as he thought about it. 'Of course! That must be the explanation!'

'There is another,' said Martin slowly. He licked his thin lips with a nervous gesture and reached for his wine. He seemed a little shrunken, as a man might look who had undergone some tremendous physical exertion, and he drank the rich fluid as though it meant life itself.

'Another explanation?' George was interested. 'What is it?'

'It may be that belief in the success of the incantation is essential for its success,' said Martin. 'The very mental doubt may have just the effect expected, a failure.

Can you understand what I am trying to say?'

'Yes,' I said, and looked at him. 'You mean that I, because of my scepticism, nullified the experiment.'

'Exactly.' Martin sipped again at his wine. 'Oh, don't think that I am throwing the blame wholly on you. I too may be at fault. It could be that a little change of inflection . . . ' He shrugged, and looked at George. 'I'm sorry, but we must be realists. No one can really say how the old Latin should sound. I have my theories but I could be wrong. I am sorry, but that is how it is.'

'Practice,' said George, and slammed his hand down onto his knee. 'We all need practice. You, John, to get rid of your doubts. You, Martin, to brush up on the speed of the incantations. Myself, to iron out the little hesitations and gaps in ritual.' He chuckled. 'No wonder we failed. How could we hope for success at the very first experiment? We must practice, all of us. Practice and practice until we are word and deed perfect. That is the only way we can ever hope for success.'

And so we practiced.

I doubt if ever men gave themselves so wholeheartedly to an aim so odd. George had decided to waste no more time and, perhaps because of his previous experiences, or perhaps that, like me, he believed in going to the source of power, the plans were now changed to call up, not a minor demon, but Satan himself.

He made changes in the ritual too.

Night was essential but lack of light was sufficient and so, when we again gathered in the big room, it was well before midnight and the streets outside were busy with people returning home from their evening pleasures. Drums too had been added, a soft, subtle, blood-stirring rhythm culled from old parchments and recorded on a tape recorder for the playback.

Other things had been changed and, when we took up our positions, it was not as three hopeful amateurs playing at wizards, but as three determined men intent heart and soul on calling up the powers of darkness.

George drew the pentagram, the five pointed star with two angles ascendant and the other pointed down. He bathed the points with blood from a canister, then set the five fat candles above the crimson points. The cabalistic symbols followed and then the outer ring of protection. Rising from his stooped position he crossed to the brazier and flung powders onto the glowing charcoal. The fires flared upward, red and green and ghastly yellow. Red tongues rose from the candles and the scent of burning incense caught my throat. I stepped forward and made the ritual gestures to the four points of the compass, to the zenith and nadir, and burned an offering of flesh and wine to the elemental spirits of earth, air, fire and water. I stepped back and took my place by the table as George, lifting his arms, spoke in rolling Latin the preliminary summons of command. As he finished I stooped and switched on the tape recorder and, as the sibilant mutter of drums echoed through the room, Martin stepped forward and, lifting his arms, began the incantation to summon the Devil.

I thought that his thin mouth was a scarlet gash spouting corruption. The words were Latin but the intonation was as the croaking of spawn from the floor of Hell. It rose with a twisted thunder of gutturals and sibilants and, mingled with it, the ceaseless pounding of the drums merged with and amplified the sound. It was just that, sound, but it was redolent with evil and primitive fears.

I felt it. I knew it, even as I wondered at the strange combination of modern and ancient represented by the tape recorder and the old incantation, I felt the hairs at the back of my neck bristle and the sweat bead my forehead with anticipation of what was to come. For now I had no doubt, no scepticism. I knew what we were doing and I knew what the incantation meant.

It was a call straight to Hell.

It was a summons to the Devil.

The drone mingled with the darkness and the darkness mingled oddly with the red tips of the candles and the leaping glow from the brazier. The pentagram became a wriggling serpent, ghastly blue in its phosphorescence, and the surrounding symbols seemed to move and shift with a life of their own. The shadows moved, the drums pounded, the thundering tones of the incantation grew louder and louder until they seemed to almost burst my skull. My eyes dimmed and strange odours assailed my nostrils.

Suddenly the pulsing began.

It shook the walls. It shook the house. It seemed to vibrate every atom in my body. It took the words of the incantation and blended with them, then emerged stronger, triumphant with added power. Smoke swirled from the brazier twisting then, as a great wind filled the room, changing into the squat and horrible shape of something that was not quite human.

Time seemed to halt, to stop so that I hung suspended on the edge of eternity then, with a blasting combination of sound and elemental forces, the pentagram dissolved into wriggling flecks of coloured light and a terrible weight crushed me down to the floor.

'John!'

Someone was shaking me. I opened my eyes and stared up at the worried features of George. I blinked at him and then at the lights.

'What happened?'

'Nothing.' He sounded bitter. 'You collapsed a moment ago and I put on the lights.'

'But I felt something,' I protested. 'George! There was something in this room, a presence. I'm sure of it.'

'Sheer self-hypnosis. The drumming, the lights, the incantation. You expected something to happen and so, to you, it did. But we've failed again.' His thin shoulders slumped in utter dejection. 'We've failed.'

'No,' I said, and even to me my voice sounded strange. 'We haven't failed. Look!'

I pointed and, as George followed my gesture, I heard the sharp intake of his breath.

'Martin! What are you doing inside the pentagram?'

He asked the question but he knew the

answer even as I did. The thing standing within the five-pointed star was not Martin. He looked the same, wore the same clothes, even his smile was the same, but his eyes belonged to nothing human. He looked at us and I shivered at the naked hate in those red eyes. He stepped forward to the edge of the pentagram, then halted as he stared at us. I shivered and fought the desire to run and keep on running away from the thing we had summoned. The thin lines of the pentagram seemed a slender defence against the forces of evil, which we had summoned into this prosaic room in a prosaic house.

'We summoned the Devil,' I said, and my voice rose until it hovered on the brink of hysteria. 'We called him and he came. But we never thought of what shape he would wear. George! In the old days didn't they use to provide a goat or something for him to enter into?'

'Yes.' George sounded as sick and as ill as I did. 'I thought that was just a part of the superstition and unnecessary for our purpose. I thought the animal was merely to provide the blood. John! What a fool I've been.'

'Steady!' I gripped his shoulders and slapped his face, hard. He calmed, and, avoiding the stare of the thing we had trapped, spoke in quieter tones:

'The explanation is simple. The person uttering the incantation attracts the powers directly to himself via the focus of the pentagram. In the old days, as you reminded me, they used to tie a goat in that focus, cut its throat and let its blood spill onto the ground. Obviously, the spirits, demons, Satan himself, can have no corporeal body such as we know it. It, they, must be an elemental web of force able to enter into and take possession of any other material body.'

He swallowed and wiped at his streaming features.

'The sacrificial victim served as a vehicle for the demon. It occupied it until it died and then had to return to its own world. But we neglected to provide such a vehicle.'

'It jumped the gap,' I said dully. 'Like an electrical spark it jumped the gap from the focus to the nearest suitable body. That was Martin. In some way it dragged Martin into the pentagram and there took possession of his body.' I stared at George. 'But Martin isn't dying. How long will Satan inhabit his body? *And how can we get rid of him?*'

The next few days were a nightmare. We had locked Martin into the room because, as George pointed out, no matter what powers Satan might have had in his free state, yet once in possession of a body he was limited by that body. A solid body cannot walk through walls even though it could cross the lines of the pentagram, and so we locked the room and settled down to a long and serious search for some way to get rid of our visitation.

Strangely enough, neither of us had any desire to ask for all the things we had thought of before the experiment. We still intended to make our demands but now, the important thing was to discover a way in which to control Satan and send him back to his own world. We culled information from mouldering tomes and tattered volumes. I added the fruit of my own labours and we assembled our armoury ready for the test of strength. As yet we had given Martin nothing in the way of food and only a little water. As George explained:

'The weaker he is physically the better chance we shall have of ridding him of his possessor. We can always nurse him back to strength afterwards.'

So we starved Martin in the hope that, by so doing, we would also weaken the thing that had taken possession of his body.

Our own armoury consisted of everything said or rumoured to be of avail against the demons of darkness. Holy Water and the Crucifix. Cold iron and silver. I had a knife inscribed with sacred runes from Scandinavia and I added it, together with a revolver loaded with silver bullets and an amulet said to contain a hair from the beard of Mohammed. George shook his head as he looked at them.

'Material weapons can only hurt the material body,' he pointed out. 'Those silver bullets could kill Martin and rob the Devil of his home, but we must avoid murder.'

'It wouldn't be murder.' I slipped the pistol in my pocket. 'Anything is justified if it means sending Satan back to his own place. Can you imagine what would happen if Martin escaped?'

'I've thought about it,' said George, and shuddered. He looked drawn and prematurely old, and I knew the weight he must have on his mind. He looked at me. 'John, I want you to let me enter that room alone. There is something I must discover and it might be dangerous.' He rested his hand on my knee. 'Please. John. Promise me that you will not interfere.'

I argued but he was insistent and in the end I had to let him go. I unlocked the door and he entered the room and, locking the door after him, I rested my ear against the panel and tried to follow what was going on inside.

I wish that I hadn't.

There were two voices, one easily recognisable as belonging to George, the other like nothing I had ever heard or dreamed of in my entire life. It was not human. It was as if an ape were chattering through the mouth of a man or, rather, as if something were trying to force human vocal chords to make sounds they were never designed to make. It slobbered did that voice, drooled, made horrible sucking noises and then, towards the last, became clear and strong as though the thing inhabiting Martin's body had finally mastered its new possession.

I sweated as I listened and my hand, as it gripped the butt of my pistol, ached from the strain. I wanted to rip open the door and send my silver bullets crashing into the owner of that vile voice. Only my promise to George and the knowledge that, if I did, I would be murdering the body of an innocent man, restrained me.

What they said in that room I shall never know. George was inside for a long, long time, and once I heard the sound of drumming and twice I caught a whiff of incense. Ugly sounds mingled with the echoes of chanting and there was the sound of threshing and movement unnatural for only two people.

When George finally came out of the room he was pale but his eyes glowed with a new enthusiasm.

I followed him up to his study and stared at him.

'Well?'

'I'm going to feed Martin,' he said. 'He's terribly weak and I promised that I would look after him.'

'You promised?' I stared hard at him and something in his expression awoke new fears within me. 'George! What happened in there?'

'Nothing.' He avoided my eyes. 'We were successful, John, that's all. We did manage to summon Satan and he's trapped in Martin's body.' He hesitated. 'He spoke to me. There are certain signs known only to the initiate and some gestures . . . ' He broke off and when he looked at me again he was defiant. 'Well, we wanted to summon him and we did. I don't know how you feel but I don't think this opportunity should be wasted. Satan promised, things . . . ' His voice faded into silence again and I felt sick with doubt as I stared at my friend.

Rumours came back to me. The ugly one of George's association with the Satanists of Devil Worshippers. He had been mixed up with them to a greater extent than I knew and now that he was confronted by the actual thing he had once worshipped! I took a deep breath. Satan was notorious for his promises and he had obviously won George over to his side. I attempted to be casual.

'Did you discover any way to send him back?'

'No. There are chants, I suppose, but we needn't worry about them now.' A fire glowed in his eyes as he looked at me. 'Think of it, John! With Satan to advise and help us we can do great things in the world. Money, power, position, the respect of others. I tell you that there is no limit to what we can achieve, John. We are standing at the threshold of a new life!'

It sounded good. It sounded too good and, even while I warmed to his enthusiasm, I was looking for the catch. Satan never gave something for nothing and I remembered Fred's warning and the fate of Sam who had finished up in a lunatic asylum hopelessly insane.

'It sounds wonderful,' I said cautiously. 'But what do we have to do for all this?'

'Nothing.'

'Nothing?'

'Well, almost nothing,' he said impatiently. 'Martin is weak and naturally Satan wants a new vehicle. We can find him one, someone young and strong, and we can make the transfer by repeating the correct incantation and making the appropriate rituals. Satan will advise us there. Then, after the transfer, we can contact those who will only be too pleased to learn of his coming. We shall form ourselves into a strong party, gain the support of the wealthy and influential, and, before long, we shall have taken over the government of this country.'

His eyes sparkled as he looked at me.

'I was right about the alternative path to knowledge, John. With the appropriate sacrifices and rituals it is possible to perform literal miracles. And there is more, much more. Satan has promised to teach me the secrets of body-transference so that, in effect, we shall be immortal. When we grow old we merely change these bodies for new ones. Think of it, John! Think of it!'

I thought of it and the more I thought of it the less I liked it. George was obviously insane. The wild promises he had heard from the thing occupying Martin's body had dazzled his reason. He no longer thought of the evil and hate, the murders and crime that would follow his so-called plan. Satan was evil and no promise he could make would be other than a tempting bribe to gain his own ends. My senses sickened as I thought of what his casual references to sacrifices and body-stealing meant. And there was another side to be considered.

We had opened a door between the worlds of material and demonic things and Satan had come through. Satan was indestructible. We could send him back but we could never destroy him and, as I thought about it, I began to have my first doubts as to whether we could send him back at all.

'Did you break the pentagram, George?'

I stared at him as I asked the question and I read my answer in his eyes. 'Why?'

'Why not?' He shrugged and attempted a laugh. 'Now that we are going to cooperate with him there was no reason to keep him locked within the pentagram. Anyway, I don't think that it would have restrained him. The longer he stays on our plane the stronger he gets and I didn't want to antagonise him.'

'I see.' I didn't tell him of my secret thoughts. Of my great fear that others would follow where Satan had led. Satan was not the only demon, merely the leader of them. Hell was filled with malignant shapes and entities, and was it not possible that they too would be eager to crowd through the opened door to acquire human bodies and to use the earth as their plaything? But it was no use telling all this to George.

I made him promise not to talk with Satan again until I returned and, on the lying excuse that I was going to search for a new vehicle for Satan, I left the house. I did not look for some unfortunate to act as a host for the thing we had called from the nether regions. Instead I went to a place I had not taken much interest in for too long.

I went to church.

The priest was intelligent, imaginative, and listened to me without interruption. I hid nothing and spoke the truth as I knew it. I did not try to justify myself nor excuse myself but made frank and open confession of what we had done. After I had finished he sat silent for a long time and then, when I had about given up hope, he nodded as if reaching a sudden decision.

'You were wise, my son, to tell me of this. For many years now the Church has fought the powers of darkness and it has not forgotten how best to subdue the evil forces. At what time shall I attend the house?'

I gave him a time, early dark, and left the church with lightened heart and freshened hope. Ridiculous? No. I had meddled in powers as old as time and needed advice and help of experts. Mother Church had fought and vanquished Satan before. I prayed that she would be able to do so again.

I knew that George had broken his promise as soon as I entered the house.

The place stank of incense and reeked of foul odours. A mumbling came from the big room, a droning and hellish chanting and the air was strained as though by tremendous forces. Softly I crept to the door and tested it. It was locked but I had a duplicate key. I did not open it but busied myself for the struggle which was to come.

I checked my revolver and slipped it into my pocket. I arranged strands of wolfbane at wrists and ankles and hung garlic around my neck. I hung the amulet around my throat and carried the rune-inscribed dagger in my left hand. The priest came just as I was finishing my preparations.

He did not deride what I had done but, after listening at the door, silently handed me a crucifix to hang over my shoulders and, uttering a prayer in rapid Latin, touched my eyes, ears, mouth and hands with Holy Water. He took his vestments from a small bag, donned his own crucifix and, with his missal in his hands, nodded to me to open the door.

We looked in at a scene direct from Hell.

George was prostrate on the polished floor and the parquet was red and sticky with blood. Flames guttered from foul-smelling candles and the thing that inhabited Martin's body was sitting on a raised chair as if it were a throne. The tape recorder was on and the air was filled with the mutter of drums and the brazier, red and lambent, filled the air with twisting tendrils of writhing smoke.

I turned off the tape recorder and switched on the lights. I quenched the brazier and kicked out the candles. Martin, or the thing which was inside of him, leapt to its feet and, from its mouth, came a horrible croaking as if it were spitting a curse.

It was answered from the corners of the room and smoke-shapes, squat and horrible, toad-like and amorphous, came hopping towards us. In the ceiling the lights dimmed as though their power was being drained away and fear, such fear as

I have never known, clogged my heart and drenched me in perspiration.

I thought that we were lost. I could not conceive of any power able to beat back those legions from hell. I shrank and, within me, my soul shrivelled as if at the touch of searing flame. Satan croaked again, triumphantly, horribly, and the shapes hopped nearer.

They recoiled as the priest began to speak sonorous Latin.

I could follow it, not all, but some, and I knew that, like Martin, the priest was speaking in vibrations rather than words. But the difference was more than that. It was as light compared to darkness, white to black, cleanliness to filth. Strong and powerful the vibrations from the Sonorous Latin filled the room with the age-old rite of exorcism and, as they felt the power of goodness flooding from the servant of God, the things from Hell quivered and shrank as though a great wind had torn away their smoke-bodies.

The lights brightened and the air cleared and only Satan himself and

George, still prostrate on the floor, faced the priest.

He advanced towards the thing on the throne, one hand outstretched and his voice rose as it gained commanding power.

'In the name of the Father, the Son and the Holy Ghost . . . '

The most potent command the world has ever known and one, which when uttered by the correct person, no force of evil could withstand.

Satan screamed!

He threshed, his eyes red pits of fury, his borrowed body writhing as he sought to fight back with all the power at his command. But he was losing and he knew it. Later, if George's plans had materialised, no ritual exorcism would have prevailed against him, but now, alone and helpless, he could do nothing to withstand the thundering command.

And then he was gone.

I felt it and the priest felt it and, to me, it was incredible that the whole world did not feel it. It was as if a cloud had passed from across the face of the sun. As if a heavy weight had been lifted from my soul and sweetness and light had been admitted to a dark and long-locked room.

For a moment Martin stood as he had during the final moments and then, falling as a tree would fall, he toppled and fell.

I caught him before he struck the floor but, even as I cradled him in my arms, I knew that Satan had taken his toll. He had taken it from George too, that poor fool who had dabbled in things too great for human understanding. I rested Martin on the floor and looked at my friend.

He stared back at me with empty eyes, his mouth drooling a little, his fingers tracing idle patterns on the floor. Like Martin his eyes were as empty as the windows of a deserted house and, like the other man, he had lost all claim to being called human.

Satan had gone, but he had taken his price with him.

Call it the soul, or the mind, or the reason. Call it what you like but I know one thing for certain. Somewhere across the thin veil which divides us from the nether regions both George and Martin writhe in eternal torment. Their bodies may die but they themselves can never die.

It is that thought which has made me old before my time and causes me to wake screaming during the night.

Because, I too, am not wholly free of blame.

3

Gift Wrapped

We don't talk about Amos Tyke now though, at one time, it seemed as if we spoke of nothing else; of how tall and handsome he was, his clothes, his car, his visitors and his dogs. He had five of them, German Shepherds that roved the house and garden, big, savage things they seemed to me.

'Of course he could be offering them for stud,' said Peggy Marsh. 'Have you ever seen anyone bringing a bitch for service, Martha?'

I hadn't and said so.

'Perhaps you didn't notice?' Peggy was insistent. 'I mean, you living so close and all.'

Susan Padbury smiled as she reached for another cookie.

'Martha would have noticed, you can bet on that. I've never known anyone's front garden needing such attention as hers has done lately.'

Which really wasn't a nice comment to have made.

Elmwood is a small community; a speculative development which misfired and which is now mainly occupied by senior citizens and the like. Frank had died before getting any real benefit from his retirement leaving me with a house too large and far too empty. It was natural that I should be interested in what went on.

'Susan's just envious,' soothed Elizabeth. 'Amos Tyke is the most interesting thing that's happened here and you're practically on his doorstep. You've met him, of course.'

'We've spoken.' I was a little curt because I hate the thought of anyone considering me a snoop.

'You have?' Elizabeth had been right; Susan was envious and it showed. 'Did he tell you anything about himself?'

'A little.'

'Don't be so bitchy, Martha,' snapped Lorna. 'You live right next to him. Now

138

tell us what you've found out.'

Lorna was older and richer than the rest of us and was the doyen of Elmwood's social life. Even so I kept her waiting while I poured coffee.

'He used to own his own business in New Mexico, something to do with electronics, but he and his wife were involved in a car accident. She died and he was hurt. They had no children and he couldn't face the old life after leaving hospital so he sold out and came here. He's rented Three Oaks for a year, but may stay longer.'

I didn't mention the way he had looked when we'd talked; how his eyes had crinkled at the corners and how the breeze had stirred his hair. And I didn't say anything about his voice, so deep, so strong and masculine.

'A widower?' Susan was thoughtful. 'Living all alone in that big house. I think it's up to us to be neighbourly. I'll invite him to a small party I'm giving next week.'

It was easy to guess why. Susan had been through two divorces and was looking for another chance. For her Amos Tyke would be a prize catch and she set about it like a general conducting a campaign. A new hairstyle, new clothes, new perfume. It was all wasted effort.

At the party Amos was coldly polite and spread himself around. The best she could manage was to get him to invite her to dinner, waving as she passed me from the bucket seat of the low, foreign convertible he drove, but that was all.

Amos Tyke, it appeared, was not socially inclined. More of a recluse than any of us had imagined. Susan claimed he had been deeply affected by the accident — a confidence he had begged her not to repeat. Or so she claimed.

But one that, if true, made the arrival of his visitors even more strange.

The first came in late September, a middle-aged woman with thick arms and hands big and red as they rested on the wheel. She drove an ageing Ford and if she was wearing her best I hate to think of what her worst could have been like. Her face was larded with cosmetics and she glared at me as she braked.

'Is this Three Oaks?'

I pruned a rose before answering. 'No. It's the next house along.'

She drove off with a grate of gears, reached the drive and vanished down it with three of the dogs loping in escort. I heard the squeal of brakes and the raucous blast of the horn. Two hours later she passed going the other way and thirty minutes after that Amos Tyke followed in his car. Curious I walked to the entrance of the drive. The dogs were nowhere to be seen.

That was the beginning. The next day another visitor arrived, a slight little thing from the orient. She stayed overnight leaving in the morning with Amos following half an hour later. Then came a three-day gap before a buxom blonde smiled at me from the confines of a battered station wagon. She smiled again when she left three hours later and, sure enough, Amos Tyke followed as before.

'Servants.' Susan was positive. 'He can't run that house on his own so he's trying to get staff. A cook, housekeeper and maybe a maid.'

'A maid for a man living alone?' Lorna raised her eyebrows. 'Well, I suppose you could call her that if you had to.'

Lorna, I've always thought, has a low mind and she took a keen pleasure in baiting Susan and her thwarted ambition. 'On the other hand, if what you told us that he told you is correct, what use would he have for a woman of any kind?'

'He was probably lying,' said Elizabeth, and smiled like a cat that has just swallowed a canary. 'Poor Susan, so gullible at times.'

Hastily I said, before an explosion could ruin our little gathering, 'If he intends hiring staff he certainly is particular. He's had a scad of visitors since the first.'

They'd arrived almost daily and had been of all shapes, ages and races. All had stayed a while then left with, invariably, Amos leaving after them.

'A marriage agency,' said Peggy flatly. 'I bet that's where they're from. Amos is looking for a wife and those women are coming to be looked over.'

If she'd tried she couldn't have insulted Susan more.

At times I think Peggy has a vicious streak. Elizabeth must have thought so too because she wasted no time pouring oil on the troubled waters.

'I don't think that's it,' she said. 'Why would a man like Amos be interested in such a wide variety? I mean, they are all so different. A man usually knows what he wants in a wife.'

'Maybe he asked for a blanket selection.' Lorna carefully selected a cookie and delicately bit into it. 'Some men are odd, you know. I think he lied to Susan to cover up some deficiency. He could be of the type needing special treatment.' She coughed, a crumb must have stuck in her throat. 'I mean, well, I've read about such things in magazines. Of course I've no actual experience. But those women could belong to a certain profession.'

I thought of his voice, the creases at the corners of his eyes, his impeccable clothing. A man like that could never be attracted to some of the creatures I had seen.

Peggy felt the same. 'There's one thing we could do,' she suggested. 'The next time a woman arrives, Martha, try to gain her friendship. Talk to her. Find out where she's from and why she's visiting.'

'And why she's leaving,' added Susan. 'You could even have a chat with Amos.'

'A good idea,' decided Lorna. 'Martha, we leave it all to you.'

I wish they hadn't. Aside from Susan's party Amos Tyke had made no effort to mingle with the community and showed no desire to do so. But I tried, using, as an excuse, concern about his dogs.

'Mrs. Tunstall,' he said, 'I can assure you your fears are groundless. You are in no danger from my dogs. They may look savage but that is what is needed in a guard dog. They are all fine animals and excellently trained. None better to protect my property. All are in fine condition as I think you will agree.'

'But expensive to keep, I imagine.'

'Not too expensive.'

'But — '

'Good day, Mrs. Tunstall.'

So much for neighbourliness. He

144

hadn't even accepted the jar of preserves I had taken along and I hadn't even seen the house. He'd met me at the end of the drive, rescued me after I'd been pinned by two of the dogs. It's little things like that which upset a woman and I think it was then that I began to dislike Amos Tyke.

Time passed. Halloween came and went and Thanksgiving loomed close. Two days before the festival a car drew up and a man rang my doorbell. Aside from salesmen and neighbours I don't get many callers, especially young men who are ill at ease. It was cold outside with a touch of frost in the air and he gratefully accepted my offer of coffee and cookies.

'Madam,' he said after lowering his cup. 'I wonder if you could help me.'

'How?'

'By answering some questions about your neighbour. The one in Three Oaks.' He saw the pursing of my lips and added, quickly, 'Let me explain. This isn't idle curiosity. The fact is I am looking for my sister, Prudence Finch. I'm Sam Finch. We share an apartment but I've been working on a project in California and only got back two days ago.' He paused then added, 'Madam, my sister has disappeared.'

'My name is Martha. I don't like to be called 'madam', I'm sorry your sister has disappeared, but what has that to do with my neighbour?'

'She came here to visit him. I've kept in touch while I was away. One of her letters — well, I guess I might as well be straight with you. Pru is fifteen years older than me and she's a little desperate at not being married. While I was around she didn't feel too bad about being single but when I left she grew lonely. So she joined a marriage agency.'

'No harm in that. Lots of people do.'

'One of the prospects was Amos Tyke,' he continued. 'Your neighbour.'

So Peggy had been right! Poor Susan!

'I know she intended to call on him and I wondered if you had seen her.' He produced a photograph. 'This is Pru.'

She had been number eighteen. I had seen her come and had seen her go. I told him so.

'Can you remember the time? It's important.'

'Early. Well before noon.'

'It figures,' he said grimly. 'Late that afternoon she was in a car showroom in Adelsburg. That's thirty miles away.' He read my expression. 'Sorry, I hadn't told you. She sold her car but the dealer was strapped for cash at the time and posted her a cheque. I found it and looked him up. He remembered the incident because not many women sell their car and leave on foot. And it went too cheap. Pru was never a fool when it came to money.'

'Was?' I met his eyes. 'Do you think she's dead?'

'If she was alive she would have contacted me by now. Are you positive you saw her leave? Did she say anything?'

'No, she just waved. I was in the garden,' I explained. 'Weeding. She blew her horn and waved as she passed.'

He said, slowly, 'Now why would she have done that?'

A question I thought about over the next few days.

Sam returned as promised. It had

grown colder and snow coated the ground and his face and hands were pinched and blue. I gave him coffee, let him get warm then said, 'Well?'

'I got the names of a couple of other women the agency had dealt with. Both had Tyke on their list of probables and both had sold their cars for half their value. I did a credit check. Neither of the women can be found. I think — '

He broke off as the phone rang. Lorna has a strident voice and I held the receiver away from my ear so Sam heard all she said. He waited until I'd hung up.

'What was that all about?'

'Just an idea I had. I got to thinking about the dogs at Three Oaks. Animals like that need a lot of meat. I was wondering who supplied it so I got the girls to phone around. There isn't a butcher or store within twenty miles who has sold so much meat on a regular order and I know he doesn't have it delivered.'

'He could pick it up himself. He drives a lot and could shop around and get his own supplies at the same time. Damn it!' Sam drove one fist into his other palm.

'Something has to be done. The trouble is we've no proof against Tyke. Every visitor he's had has left his house and he can call on you as a witness to prove it. The fact three have vanished after selling their cars need have nothing to do with him.'

'The police?'

'I've tried but they weren't interested. I can't blame them. Pru could just have taken off and I can't even be certain the other two women ever called on Tyke. I'm sure in my mind that Tyke is guilty, but the police won't act without proof.'

Linda Carson helped us to get it.

She came as Sam was about to leave, driving an ancient car that moved slowly up the road, skidding and slithering on the snow. It stopped outside and a woman climbed out and stood looking helplessly from side to side. Sam grunted and headed for the door. I followed.

'Can you help me?' The woman appealed to Sam as he approached. 'I'm looking for Three Oaks. Is it close?'

'It's the next house down the road.'

'Oh, good. I'd lost my way and never thought I'd find it.' She had a soft voice and was thirty-plus. A tall creature with a smooth face, wide-spaced eyes and good teeth. 'I'm Linda Carson,' she said as I drew near. 'Isn't it dreadful weather?'

I nodded. Her hair was bleached and there was a hardness about her eyes which belied the softness of her voice. She glanced past me to my house then up the road to where the drive to Three Oaks was almost invisible in the thickening darkness. 'Have you lived here long?'

'Several years.'

'Then you must know Amos Tyke?'

'Of course. Are you visiting him?'

'Yes. Has he lived here long? Does he own the house?'

Another prospect, I thought grimly, sounding out the neighbours before actually meeting the interested party. Even so she was entitled to a warning, but before I could give it she reached and entered her car.

Back in the house Sam turned towards me. 'Martha! This could be our chance! Dress warm, get something to hit with and let's follow her.'

'Visit, you mean?'

'Why not?' Impatiently he added, 'For all we know that woman is in danger. At least we can tell her about my sister and the others.'

'The dogs?'

'You said they weren't around for long after a visitor arrived. They only ran loose when Tyke was away or locked up in the house after he'd returned. If they come at us we'll drive them off. Have you a gun?'

Frank had owned a twelve-gauge, more to be one of the boys than for any real intention of killing things, but I'd kept it wrapped in oiled cloth and stacked it together with some cartridges in a wardrobe. I dug it out and handed it to Sam who fussed over it while I found a heavy poker. Muffled, armed, we headed towards Three Oaks and Amos Tyke.

A car came down the road as we reached the sidewalk and, sure enough, it slowed to allow an arm to wave through the open window. Behind it I could see the round, blonde head of Linda Carson.

'Damn! We're too late.' Sam stared after the car, frowning. 'Why should she be driving with the window open in this weather?'

'Some people do.'

'Maybe. Well, never mind, we still have time to catch Amos Tyke. Let's go!'

I don't know what we expected to find. The only positive danger was the dogs but as we walked up the drive we saw no sign of them and that was all to the good. Neighbours don't shoot each other's dogs but, had the beasts attacked, Sam, wound up as he was, would have let fly. As things turned out we reached the door of the house without incident. He stopped me as I reached for the bell.

'No,' he whispered. 'Let's give him a surprise.'

I hoped we wouldn't get one instead but before I could say anything Sam had opened the door. I followed him close, nose and eyes tingling to a sharp acrid smell. I'd been inside the house before when old Joshua Klien had been alive and so knew my way about. The big living room was empty and cold enough to turn our breath into vapour. No wonder Linda Carson had cut short her visit — husband-hungry or not there were limits.

On the long table, standing in a scatter of sawdust, was a square box neatly wrapped in gift paper and tied with a wide, red ribbon. A white address label stood out against the bright paper but it was blank.

'Martha!' Sam stepped forward as I set down the poker and pulled at the ribbon. 'You can't do that!'

'Why not?' The paper rustled as I pulled it free. 'Where is Amos Tyke? Does this house feel to you as if it's lived in? Now you keep watch while I see what we have here. And remember the dogs.'

Under the paper was a plastic box sealed with adhesive tape. I pulled it free, threw it aside, lifted the box and tipped it over. A shower of sawdust streamed over the table and then, as I shook the box, something big and roughly round.

'God!' Sam stepped back raising the shotgun. 'What the hell is that?'

It was Linda Carson, but it couldn't be. We both had seen her leave waving from the open window of her car, and it was impossible that she should have left her head behind, but that's what lay on the table, blonde hair and all. At first I thought it had to be a bust and then I knew it wasn't. No sculptor goes to the trouble of showing severed arteries, windpipe and spinal column in the base of the neck and the colours were as real as life. Sam reached out and touched it and I heard the shudder of his breath.

'Cut,' he said. 'Sliced by something incredibly sharp then treated so that it feels like rubber. And the eyes! Look at the eyes!'

They were open, calm, the whole face tranquil.

'Where's Tyke?' Sam turned, glaring, shotgun poised. 'Where is the murdering swine?'

'Careful, Sam,' I warned. 'Put down that gun.'

'Like hell I will. Tyke murdered my sister! He's going to pay for it. Where is he?'

A door led from the living room to the cellar. As Sam yelled the question Amos Tyke stepped through it into the living room. He held something in his hand. As he levelled it Sam fired the shotgun emptying both barrels at point-blank range.

Amos Tyke fell backwards, the impact of the charge splitting him open so that his insides could be seen. They were all bright and shining and nothing like what you'd expect to find beneath a human skin. Looking at him all I could think of was a busted watch.

Then more shots as Sam took care of the dogs.

Later, after the authorities had done what had to be done, Sam and I figured what it must have been all about.

'Tyke wanted victims,' he said, sitting in my best chair before the fire.

'The visitors. Poor bitches yearning for a better life. You saw them come and you saw them go. In so doing you gave Amos Tyke a perfect alibi.'

I poured him another glass of bilberry wine.

'Only you didn't really see them go. You saw something wearing their clothes, a mask, a wig. A dim figure that waved in passing and your memory and imagination completed the rest. There was no reason for you to suspect they had been murdered for the sake of their heads. Their clothing was dumped or given to charity. The dogs took care of the rest.'

'And selling the cars?'

'That was to kill the trail. An abandoned car would give rise to questions but one legally sold would leave no trace. My guess is there are a string of agencies who bought cars cheaply from women they thought to be genuine and real. Amos followed in order to pick up the impostor. Hidden in the trunk of his car no one would see it return to Three Oaks.

'It,' he repeated. 'Another alien. There had to be two of them.'

A dual operation and the reason why Amos Tyke had been so unapproachable and socially aloof. It made sense once you knew about it. But — ?

There was no need to ask the question. There had been enough electronic equipment in the thing Sam had shot to have included a radio or alarm device of some kind.

Its companion had been warned. Human or not it had vanished or, if it had been found, those concerned were keeping quiet about it.

As we had been ordered to keep quiet.

But you can't stop thinking. After Sam had gone and I was alone again I had plenty of time to think. Of the head we had found and how it had been processed. Of the address which might have been written on the label. Of the dogs and how they had been fed.

Female human heads — what kind of a market could there be for such trophies? Where could that market be? What purpose could they serve? What use? Items for display? Toys for alien children? Gifts to be won in competition? Presents certainly.

Why else should the box have been gift-wrapped?

I wish that Amos Tyke had never come to Elmwood because now I have a craven fear of dogs and, at night, the stars are filled with menace.

4

The Dolmen

Basil Heather came to the parish of Millhaven with firm ideas about quashing all the country nonsense he was convinced occupied most of the thoughts of his parishioners. A bustling, officious man of medium height and round girth with a glint in his eyes and determination in the set of his jaw, he was of the modern school who believed in nothing that they could not touch or see. Aside from orthodox religion, of course, and even in that he had little patience with those who wished to argue theology.

The parish, however, had been spoiled by Dr. Wenton, Heather's predecessor who had been lenient almost to the point of idiocy, or so Heather thought when he came to look over his new living. Funds that should have been earmarked for a new organ or the restoration of the roof of the small but agreeably old church, had been squandered on Morris Dances and similar stupidity which everyone of intelligence knew to be connected with the old, pre-Roman worship. Indeed, the debt of the parish was such that any other man might well have thrown up his hands and let things ride while waiting for a dispensation from providence or, far more likely, a bequest in the will of some of the local gentry.

However, there he was and in Millhaven he meant to stay.

He was not married but he employed a housekeeper, a gardener and occasionally hired a chauffeur driven car. He took complete possession of the vicarage and in a short while had taken complete possession of the village and its various activities too. These he reorganised with the main object in mind of reducing the debt of the church and laid out a complete programme of whist drives, benefits, amateur theatricals and raffles which would have kept a village three times the size of Millhaven busy for the best part of a year.

Unfortunately, as he soon began to realise, no one, not even the most energetic vicar, can obtain blood from a stone or money from those who haven't got it, and it was forced upon him that he had to find some other solution to the problem.

Inevitably he thought of the local legend.

About two miles from the village, set on a rolling slope of the downs, was an old dolmen, which had been there ever since the villagers could remember. Indeed, it was said that it had been there before the Romans came and was the burial site of the old chiefs who had fallen in battle. Heather, while not disputing the legend, had his own ideas that were supported by the Squire, bluff Sir Welby of Welby Hall, the local magistrate and the authority on everything in the vicinity. Over a bottle of rare port to which he had been invited Heather mentioned the subject on his mind.

'The Dolmen?' Welby nodded. 'Of course I know it. Know all about it too I dare say. Pre-Roman I'd swear to it.

Possibly connected up with the old Druids and some of their sacrifices or other tomfoolery. What makes you ask?'

'I've heard that it is a burial mound or community grave of the old chieftains,' said Heather thoughtfully. 'I'm inclined to believe that is true. In such a case it would be worth excavating the mound to discover whether there are any works of art or weapons or things of intrinsic or historical value there. The old burial customs used to insist that a chief be buried with his jewellery and eating utensils.' He sipped at his port. 'It would be interesting to excavate the mound to discover its exact date.'

'Don't do it,' said Welby promptly. 'Leave well alone, that's my motto and that's what I always do. We like the Dolmen the way it is, don't want a lot of foreigners coming here to dig it up. Why, it's a landmark for miles around . . . useful when on the hunt.'

To the Squire as to the rest of the villagers anyone not born in the parish was a foreigner. Heather had been uncomfortably aware that he was so classed but, because of his cloth and calling, he had been given a special sort of dispensation as it were so that it was tacitly assumed that he was Millhaven born and bred by adoption if not by fact.

'So you advise against it, Squire?'

'I do,' said Welby firmly. 'Have some more port.'

Heather followed the suggestion but did not take the advice. As he needed the support, both financial and moral, of the Squire he did not press the point about excavating the Dolmen but retired to find fresh guns to bear on the old man's prejudices. He found them in the nature of old parchments, which, quite by accident, he found between the leaves of an old missal tucked away in the study. The next time he and the Squire met he was armed with new information.

'About the Dolmen,' he said as soon as they were seated. 'I've found some papers which gives me reason to believe that certain treasure was buried there at the time of the Dissolution. There used to be a monastery about here, I understand, and they hid much of their plate and vessels to save them from the ministers of King Henry VIII.' He carefully folded his parchment. 'See? It states quite plainly that certain items were buried at the site of the Dolmen.'

'And dug up again later, no doubt,' said the Squire. 'But I'm glad that you brought that paper with you. I have one of my own in the library and it should interest you.'

He rose and, with much muttering and fumbling about, returned with a cracked and seared scrap of paper yellowed with age and brittle with time. Heather took it with the respect he had for anything very old and carefully unfolding it read the crabbed writing which covered it.

'It seems very clear,' he said thoughtfully. 'In Latin, of course, but that presents no problem. I majored in Latin as one of the subjects of my B.A.' The explanation given and the old man suitably impressed he returned to his reading.

'This seems to be an account of a predecessor of yours as to what was supposed to have taken place at the Dolmen about three hundred years ago.'

He read on, his lips moving as he translated the crabbed writing. 'A coven of witches was suspected to assemble there and to perform wild and unnatural rites to the general disturbance of the peace. A raid was made and two men and three women arrested, later tried for witchcraft, and publicly burned at the stake.' He looked at the Squire. 'Superstition and the account of a clerk with an inflamed imagination.'

'Read on,' said Webly comfortably. 'The last part is more interesting.'

Heather read on, slightly embarrassed by his host's own knowledge of the dead language. When he had read to the end he snorted and put down the paper.

'So strange things were supposed to have happened in the disturbers of that Dolmen. After the trial it was decided to destroy the stone and a barrel of gunpowder was used for the purpose. It failed but the explosion injured ten men. A second attempt also failed but this time the crops failed, the cows ran dry, and strange manifestations terrified the village. There was no third attempt and, as far as we know, the Dolmen has been left undisturbed unto this day.'

'Correct,' said Welby. 'And I say that it's best left alone.'

Heather sighed and began the hard task of convincing the old man that he was both out of date and hopelessly stupid. It is not surprising that both men began to lose their tempers.

'Say what you wish, Squire, but I intend to excavate that mound. If you refuse to help me then I shall appeal to the village.'

'You'll get no help from them,' snapped the old man. 'They know better than to mess about with things best left alone. You're new here so you wouldn't understand, but I'll take a bet that you won't get a single man to help you.'

'I shall shame them into helping me,' said Heather firmly. 'It isn't as if I want them to actually do anything but obey my orders. Once they shift the stone I can continue with the excavations myself.'

Welby brightened and smiled for the first time since the argument had begun.

'That might not be so bad then. As I

understand it the curse applies only to the actual disturber of the Dolmen, so you won't be really loosing any trouble on the parish if you take it all on yourself.'

'Curse?' Heather sighed. 'Not another of those stupid legends.'

'You can call it stupid,' said Welby darkly. 'But I for one wouldn't like to bring it upon myself.'

Heather had some difficulty in restraining himself. He reminded the Squire that this was, after all, the twenty-first century and not the dark ages and repeated his determination to have the stone shifted as soon as he could arrange to do so. Shortly after he took his leave and it was not until he was almost home that he remembered that he had neglected to inquire as to the precise nature of the curse. He dismissed it from his mind as being of no possible importance and spent the next few days gathering as much information about the Dolmen as he could.

Two weeks later the work was begun, everyone taking the utmost care so that the great stone should not be damaged in any way. The vicar told himself and others that he was not a vandal. Nevertheless it was a sullen group of men that assembled at the site and began to dig away the dirt from around the edge of the stone. Only his searing remarks from the pulpit and his personal assurance that he would hold himself responsible for any curse or malignant manifestations had persuaded them to agree to do the task at all.

The work was long and arduous and needed plenty of patience. At first Heather had hoped that the local breakdown wagon would be able to lift the stone and swing it to one side with its crane, but, after one glance at the stone, the owner had emphatically stated that the crane big enough to move that weight hadn't yet been mounted on wheels. He did, however, offer the loan of several bars and wedges and promised that, when the dirt had been cleared away, he would see what could be done to topple it over.

Heather himself was full of enthusiasm. Already he could see the big write-ups in the illustrated papers of the wonderful finds he would make and he toyed with the idea of presenting some odd work of art to the British Museum with, naturally, his name attached as donor. Second thoughts however persuaded him that it would be financially better for the village to have its own museum attached to the excavated site. Postcards would be sold and a souvenir booklet of which he had already made a rough draft. The income would be small but surely enough to keep the church once and for all out of debt. His own rewards would automatically come with the preferment his success would deserve.

After two weeks of steady digging the men announced that it would be dangerous to continue and Heather sent for the garage proprietor and warned him to bring his heaviest and strongest breakdown wagon. The warning was unnecessary, the man only had the one, but he arrived at the site shortly after receiving the telephone message and, with himself supplying the knowledge and Heather the unwanted supervision, he readied everything for the toppling over of the stone.

Dirt was scraped away from beneath

each end and strong cables passed beneath and around the mass of granite. The wagon was backed and the cables fitted. Men were stationed with bars and wedges to thrust beneath the lifted edge and, when everything was ready, the owner climbed into his vehicle and slowly drove forward.

A shout from the watching men warned that the stone was lifting and they thrust in their wedges. The engine of the wagon roared, dirt plumed from beneath the wheels, and one of the cables parted with the sound of a cracking whip.

That it missed decapitating the vicar was something the villagers never understood. He had stooped at that very moment and, just before he straightened, the broken end of the thick cable lashed the air just above his head. Had it made contact Heather would have lost all interest in matters earthly. Even as it was, pale and shaken at the near escape, he did no more than chide the garage owner for faulty equipment and suggest that perhaps it would be better if some other method was attempted.

The garage owner, without mentioning the cost of the ruined cable, agreed, and rigged up a double-strength chain attached to a grapnel. Warning everyone to stand clear he drove forward again and, as the scene of burning rubber from his spinning tyres filled the twilight, the men yelled encouragement as they thrust home their wedges.

'Good,' smiled the vicar proudly as he examined the widening gap. 'One more good pull should see the job finished.'

He smiled around at the men and promised them all a treat if they would stick at the task. He knew that, once they had a chance to think about it and to consider the story, his near miss would be interpreted as a direct sign of malign powers. As he hoped the prospect of free beer persuaded them to get the job over and done with and, as the engine strained and the men sweated, the great stone slowly toppled from where it had lain for untold centuries into the new bed prepared for it.

The only other damage at that time was the total loss of the chain, which, caught beneath the mass of granite, could not be salvaged.

Beneath the stone was a flat slab of some strange substance resembling slate, which was firmly set into the ground. Heather examined it, quivering with eagerness to discover what was beneath, but it was late and the men were restless and he decided to put off further investigations until the next day. Besides, he would rather examine the treasure, which he was convinced lay beneath the slab, without witnesses. Gossip was rife in the village and he had no desire for awkward questions to be asked concerning the fate of some jewelled object of rare worth or other items of a similar nature. The vicar, in everything including his religion, was of an intensely practical turn of mind.

There was a message waiting for him when he returned to the vicarage after seeing to the rewarding of his helpers. Sir Welby answered the phone and coughed as Heather introduced himself.

'Just rang to find out whether you were all right, Heather,' he said gruffly. 'Are you?'

'Of course I'm all right. What makes you think I'm not?'

'Just my curiosity,' murmured the Squire. 'I heard about that accident you almost had. Rather nasty thing, what?'

'It was an accident,' said the vicar sternly. 'I am fully aware that gossip will try and make something supernatural out of it, but it was plainly due to a bad cable.'

'Of course,' said the old man hastily. 'Never said it wasn't, still, you never know.' He coughed again. 'By the way, if you should need me, just give me a ring. I've an extension on my bedside table and I could be with you in ten minutes.'

The vicar made short work of that suggestion. When he put down the telephone he was certain that the old Squire must have long passed his prime and be well on the road to senile decay. He also decided to draft out a series of sermons ridiculing superstition and those who should know better than to spread such nonsense. The Squire, while a person of some importance in the community, should learn that times changed and that there was no room for the old village nonsense.

When he finally put out the light and went to bed Heather was busy compiling, mentally at least, the preface to his proposed booklet describing the trouble he had had with local prejudice before he could excavate the site beneath the stone.

He was awakened in the night by what first he thought was the patter of rain against his window pane but, as he came more fully to his senses, he recognised it as a kind of snuffling sound, the kind of sound an animal would make. At the same time he was conscious of a terrific din from the village. It seemed that every dog for miles around was barking with a frenzied madness as if they were frightened or angry at something.

Rising, the vicar crossed to the window and looked out. From his vantage point, his room was on the second storey of the vicarage, he could see most of the village spread out before him. Lights shone in most windows and the harsh voices of men trying to control their dogs increased rather than diminished the noise. It wasn't raining and Heather was at a loss to account for what had made the noise at his window, when he became aware of something staring at him.

He looked up sharply just in time to catch a glimpse of a shadowy shape flit away into the night and, together with its going, the dogs ceased their barking and quieted down. The sudden jangling of the telephone made the vicar jump.

'Is that you, Heather?' said old Welby. 'Just thought I'd call to see if everything was all right. Did you hear the noise?'

'Yes, it's died down now.' Heather forced himself to remember that the old man meant well. 'But it wasn't that which woke me.' He described the noises he had heard at the window.

Welby was silent for a long time and when he spoke his words didn't make sense to the vicar, now shivering with the cold and thinking longingly of his warm bed.

'Dogs. They used to bury dogs with the chiefs in the old days. Or ravens? Could it have been ravens?'

Heather slammed down the receiver.

174

The next day he collected a couple of crowbars, a heavy hammer, a rucksack and a pick and shovel and had the garage owner drop him and his load off at the side of the stone.

There were a few lookers-on hanging about, none of them too near, and the vicar had the unpleasant feeling that they were waiting for something to happen to him rather than waiting to see what he was going to do. He ignored them and, scraping away the dirt around the edges of the strange slab, began to lever with the crowbars until he felt something yield.

As it did so there was a terrible crack of thunder from the sky and a wind blew across the downs with such force that it almost blew the vicar's hat from his head.

'Confounded storm coming up,' he muttered. 'At least it will keep the others away from the site. I wish that I'd remembered to bring a raincoat.'

For a moment he hesitated between continuing his excavations or returning to the vicarage for his raincoat. However, that would have meant a five mile walk and consequent loss of time and the vicar was not a patient man. So he redoubled his efforts and finally, after much groaning and reluctance, the slab tilted up, there to be propped by a convenient piece of rock.

Heather looked down into utter darkness.

'Faugh!' He turned his head to avoid the dank, stale odour that came welling upwards toward him. 'This must be the burial chamber. That air must have been trapped down there for two thousand years.'

He didn't stop to remember that burial mounds did not have burial chambers as such but were merely dirt and stone piled onto the dead. He didn't think it strange either that the Dolmen wasn't a true dolmen as such but was merely an unsupported slab of granite. More like a weight than anything else and certainly not a religious structure.

He peered into the darkness again and this time ventured to light a match. It went out immediately and so did a second.

'It will take time to let that bad air

clear,' he said thoughtfully. He glanced up at the sky. 'That storm is coming nearer. I wonder if I have time to get home and return before it breaks?'

Another rumble of thunder decided him and, after making quite certain that there was no one about whom he could send on an errand, he decided to tackle the five mile walk. Not, as he told himself, that it would be time wasted. The ninety minutes or so necessary for the double journey would enable the stale air in the vault to be cleared and, as it was so dark down there, he would return with a flashlight. A short examination today to discover any jewelled objects or similar works of like value, and he would invite old Welby for an inspection tomorrow. At least, his find would convince the old man that he knew what he was talking about.

Heather was quite jubilant as he strode across the downs and not even the warning drops of rain pattering on his black hat dampened his enthusiasm.

He had a little trouble finding his torch and there was a message from his bishop and another from a parishioner who had an urgent matter to discuss. These things took time, the parishioner proved unexpectedly difficult, and it was not until a couple of hours had passed that the vicar could make his way back to the site. It was raining by then, cold sheets of penetrating rain, which drove every sensible man indoors and even sent the birds huddling on their branches.

Dressed in his raincoat and filled with curiosity as to what he would find the vicar made light work of the rain. Also, if the truth were known, it wasn't just curiosity which drove him. He was filled with the fear that someone might lower himself down into the vault before he returned and there was no knowing what damage might be done or what items stolen.

The vicar, even though he was a newcomer to the parish, had quite managed to convince himself that the Dolmen and all it contained was his personal property — to be used to pay off the church debt, of course, but by himself and none other.

He almost ran the last few hundred

yards to the site and when he reached it could have cried out at what he saw.

Someone had closed the slab again.

It must have been deliberate, he distinctly remembered propping it up with a piece of rock, and he felt a sudden fear that someone had emptied the tomb before him. This ungenerous thought was replaced by another as he looked around for the tools he had brought with him. Suppose someone had lowered themselves down into the chamber and the slab had then fallen shut behind them? It was possible, an accidental knock could have dislodged the rock, and, as he remembered, the stone slab was far too heavy to be pushed up from within.

Hastily he looked for a crowbar.

He had trouble finding one. The same malicious person who had shut the slab had, for reasons of his own, scattered the tools far and wide. The vicar had a hard job locating even one of them and when he finally found a crowbar it was in a bush some three hundred yards from where he had left it. He decided to be very firm with the person responsible and, perspiring freely inside his raincoat, he set to work once again on the slab.

This time, when he had managed to lift it, he threw it right over so that it couldn't possibly be closed by accident again. Dropping the crowbar he knelt at the edge of the opening and called down to whoever was inside.

'Hello, there! Are you hurt?'

His voice echoed and rolled and came back to him strangely distorted. He tried again.

'This is Heather, the vicar, can you hear me?'

He waited until the echoes died away then, taking his torch from his pocket, shone it into the opening.

About ten feet below him he saw something white and ghastly familiar. He had attended enough burials to have become inured to the thought of death but there was something about the pitiful heap of bones below which upset him. The emotion lasted but a moment for, as he reminded himself, what else could he have expected in a burial chamber but bones?

He looked again, shining the light about the chamber but aside from the skeleton he saw nothing but a round hole in one side of the vault. Obviously this was merely the ante-chamber or outside vault and the skeleton was that of a slave set to guard the outer portal. So the vicar told himself and gained some comfort from it.

Thunder burst overhead as he stared into the vault and the rain began to come down with redoubled force. For a moment he considered the possibilities of dropping down into the vault and having a look at the treasures, which must undoubtedly lie down the tunnel. He considered it, then reluctantly gave up the idea. Getting down was no problem but the floor was ten feet down and if he lowered himself into the chamber he doubted his ability to climb out again.

As no one knew that he was at the site and as it was terrible weather and getting on towards sunset, it was quite possible that, if he trapped himself, he would have to stay there the entire night.

Slowly he straightened and considered

what best to do. He could replace the slab, he supposed, and that would keep the chamber dry. It would also discourage whoever it was who had tampered with it before. On the other hand it would waste more time but, as he would need a ladder and other things, he could get the garage owner to come out in his wagon and help him.

The decision made, the vicar levered at the stone until he had manoeuvred it back into its original position. Then, after a last glance around, he began to make his long way home.

He became aware of the presence shortly after he had left the site. It seemed to hover all around him like an evil cloud and, as he walked, he became aware again of the same peculiar snuffling as had wakened him the previous night.

Imperceptibly he lengthened his stride and, at the same time, looked around him for a familiar form. The downs were deserted, the rain filling the air with mist, and he seemed to walk alone in a world of his own.

He had walked a long time before

something loomed up before him and, to his surprise, he found that he was back at the site of the disturbed stone.

'Strange,' he said. 'I must have walked in a circle. It must have been the mist.'

It upset him a little but not much for, as everyone knows, it is very easy to walk in a circle if there are no familiar landmarks to steer by. Desert travellers do it all the time and people have often done it when thinking of other matters. So, at least, the vicar told himself but his peace of mind was rudely shattered when, after an hour's walk, he found himself back in the same place once more.

This time he sat down to rest awhile and, as he sat, he became aware of the presence more strongly than before. He shook himself, angry at the thoughts filling his mind and, tired as he was, he set out once more through the rain and the thickening dusk towards the village.

He walked with greater care this time, watching where he was going and trying not to imagine that something was following his every step. It wasn't easy to do that because the snuffling sound had grown louder and joined with it was a peculiar rustling as if something huge and invisible were marching at his side.

Heather glanced towards the sound, narrowing his eyes as he stared at the darkening mist, and vaguely, he thought he could see a monstrous shape walking beside him. It was terrible that shape, so terrible that he forgot his discipline and impatience at the old beliefs and began to run hard towards the safety of the village, to the bright lights at home and to the sound of the old Squire's calm voice.

He ran until his legs ached and he could hardly breathe and then, when he was near to collapse, he felt his foot catch on something and he went sprawling on hands and knees.

Somehow he wasn't surprised to find that he was lying across the slab back at the site of the huge stone.

He sprawled and fought for breath while, all the time, a little primitive part of his mind was screaming a warning to get up and run.

He tried and struggled to his feet. He even took a step away from the stone then, as a great shadow loomed above him, he tilted back his head and screamed at the top of his lungs.

The scream was cut off as though with a knife.

A labourer, wending his tired way home from a hard day in the fields heard the scream and, muttering something under his breath, tucked in his elbows and ran towards the village. Later, after he had fortified himself at the bar of the inn, he went up to see the old Squire and the two of them sat for a long while in talk. Afterwards the labourer denied he had heard anything at all.

The Squire, as soon as the night had passed and it was day, saddled his horse and went for a ride. It was possibly by sheer chance that he rode towards the site of the Dolmen.

It wasn't the same as it had been the day before.

The great stone, moved with so much time and effort, dragged and toppled from its age-old bed, had somehow been replaced.

The Squire looked at it for a long time

then, slowly dismounting, he walked towards it and spent a long time examining its base. He kicked a heap of dirt over something he saw and then, his seamed old face serious, he mounted and rode back to the village.

Some men came out afterwards and shovelled dirt back into the place they had taken it from. Some of them even shovelled dirt high around the base of the stone as if they wanted to be certain that every crack and gap was filled. Only when they were satisfied that all was as it had been did they return to the village.

For a while there was talk about the missing vicar but it soon died because no one had really liked him and, as the Squire was also the magistrate, they left it to him to decide what official action, if any, should be taken.

None ever was.

The Squire made a report to the Church Authority and as far as anyone knew, Heather had just run away one day and never returned.

But the Squire spent some time reading an old parchment, a companion to the one Heather had laughed at, and what he read seemed to satisfy him that everything was in order. He would have warned the vicar more than he had done but for the man's laughter and scorn. For what modern man could conceive of a burial vault for something not of this earth? Old powers had trapped it, chained it, and sealed the tomb with a human sacrifice. That same power had resealed the burial vault after the vicar had so unwisely opened it after so many years.

It was only poetic justice that he, in his turn, should have served as the living victim necessary to seal the vault.

They have a new vicar at Millhaven now. He is a simple, quiet old man who spends much of his time in the garden and plays chess with the Squire and a few of his cronies. He doesn't interfere with the village in any way and doesn't worry about the church debt. He has only visited the Dolmen once, and that was after a long talk with the Squire. They went out early one Sunday before anyone was about and what they did didn't take very long.

It was a simple service, not quite the thing Heather would have chosen had he been able, but, as the Squire said, he couldn't possibly grumble about the size of his monument.

He even placed a few wild flowers over the spot where he had seen a shred of black protruding past the stone, a scrap of material of the sort of which clerical raincoats are made.

But the Squire was glad he had arranged for the burial service.

He thought that Heather would have appreciated it.

5

Time and Again

There were times when Kelough was firmly convinced that Professor Pierre Denislov laboured under the delusion that he was God. If so he had reason. The man had power; as Head of the Terminal Studies Institute he could make or break a career at whim. He had authority; as one of the world's leading surgeon psychiatrists his work on the function of the brain was accepted as gospel. And he had the arrogance of a man who has so often been right that he had forgotten the few times when he had been wrong.

He also had the appearance, Kelough thought as, entering Denislov's office, he walked over an acre of carpet towards his desk. The professor leaned back in his chair as he approached. He was a big man with a balding head and his deep-set eyes and hooked nose gave him the appearance of a brooding eagle. His hand tapped restlessly at the newspaper spread across his desk.

Kelough knew what the banner-headlines proclaimed. Inwardly he braced himself for the blast. Instead Denislov said quietly, 'It seems that someone has been talking, Roger. I know you well enough to know that you are not responsible. Brenner?'

'I don't know.' Kelough was too honest to throw the blame on another without proof. 'It could have been, he was sore when you fired him, but what would he hope to gain?'

'Notoriety, perhaps?' Denislov thrust aside the newspaper. 'Revenge? Not that it matters now. The light of public attention has been thrown on our work here and it is now important to minimize the wild speculation at present rife in the press. You will attend to it.'

God, thought Kelough, handing down the tablets, but he was being unfair. As liaison officer it was his job to pacify the press. The Institute, for all its academic weight, didn't run to the expense of a

Public Relations Office. Not for the first time he regretted the economy.

'All right,' he said. 'I'll do what I can. I'll — '

'That has already been attended to,' interrupted Denislov curtly. 'I have arranged that a representative of the press will attend you here. I specified someone with minimal intelligence so it should not be hard for you to communicate the seriousness of our work and the importance of accurate and unemotional valuation. You will show the person around, explain what has to be explained, put things in their proper perspective and dissipate any wild rumours. If we are to be subjected to the attentions of the press I would prefer that they print the truth rather than the idiotic nonsense in which they at present indulge.'

'That may be easier said than done,' said Kelough drily. 'How far can I go? They mention the Capsule, do I show that? And how about your own work? You said that you wanted to wait before making an announcement. Now that the beans have been spilled we might as well come clean.'

Denislov nodded. 'True.'

'Then you give me a free hand?'

'Naturally, I trust you, Roger. I am sure that you will not let me down.'

Which meant, Kelough knew, that not only did things have to be as before but the Institute had to be shown in a better light than ever.

Back in his own office his secretary lifted her head as he cane through the door.

'A moment, Doctor,' she said. 'There's a person to see you. Someone from the press, a reporter, I think.'

'So soon?' Kelough frowned. 'By appointment?'

'Yes, Doctor.'

They had worked fast, thought Kelough as he made his way to the inner office. Predators scenting newly-killed meat would have moved as fast and for the same reason. Both they and the press liked to be in at the death.

★ ★ ★

A girl waited inside. She was tall with blonde hair neatly tied in a plait which hung over one shoulder. Her dress fitted close and stopped an eye-catching distance above the knees. Her stockings were sheer and her shoes matched her bulky handbag, little gilt buckles catching and reflecting the light. She stared at him with a dazed expression and then shook her head.

Kelough glanced around the office. 'Something wrong?'

'No, of course not. It was just that I had the most odd feeling that I had seen you before.' Her voice was deep and musical. 'That I had lived through the whole sequence before. Odd, isn't it?'

'Odd but not uncommon. It happens all the time and mostly when you are young. Déjà vu, they call it. The 'already seen'. Surely you've experienced it before?'

He smiled as she nodded. 'There you are, then. Cigarette?'

'Thanks.' Through the smoke she looked at him and said, 'This déjà vu — is there an explanation for it?'

'There are explanations for everything,' he said dryly. 'In this case the most common is that you see a thing, immediately forget it and then resee it. Ridiculous, of course. If you forget it how would you know that you had previously seen it?'

'One false explanation bites the dust,' she said, smiling. 'And the true answer?'

'No one knows. I mean that, literally no one knows, all we can do is to guess. The only thing we are sure of is that it happens.' His eyes drifted from her face to her shoes and back again. 'As an inquisitor you are rather exceptional. Do they always send a pretty girl on these assignments?'

'If there is one available, yes.'

'Why?'

Her smile widened. 'Doctor Roger Kelough, a once-practicing psychiatrist and now closely associated with the famous Professor Denislov, a clever and brilliant young man, to ask such a question. Come now, Doctor, you know the answer.'

'A young and charming, not to say

extremely attractive female, can prise secrets from crusty old academics where a man would fail. And the name is Roger.'

'Sue Weston.' She held out her hand. 'Pleased to meet you.'

'The pleasure is mine.'

'I wonder — ' She looked at him thoughtfully. 'You can't really be enjoying this. No one likes to be investigated and have to defend themselves.'

'Against such an adversary, it is a pleasure.'

'You're gallant,' she said. 'Or cunning. I can't decide which. But flattery will get you nowhere.'

Kelough shrugged. 'At least they didn't send a team. You must carry a lot of weight with your agency.'

'I do, but not that much. I'm alone because the professor insisted on it and he carries quite a bit of high-level influence.' She became serious. 'Even so that influence won't help him if half of what is rumoured is true. The public will stand a lot in the name of scientific research but what has been hinted is too grisly even for them. Do you really kill people to order?'

'No.'

'So you let them die then by witholding medical assistance?'

'No.'

'Then is it true that you have proven the reality of reincarnation?'

'No.' He smiled. 'You don't seem to be getting anywhere, do you?' Before she could answer he touched a button of the intercom. 'Mary? Order two coffees, please. One black and the other — ?' He looked at Sue, who held up her thumb. 'Two of the same and right away, please.'

Over the coffee he got down to business. 'Let's get one thing perfectly clear. This is the Institute of Terminal Studies. It isn't a hospital. It isn't a geriatric institution. We are not concerned here with keeping people alive. Understood?'

She nodded. 'Then what do you do?'

'Exactly what the name implies. We study people who die.' He leaned back in his chair and chose his words with care, conscious of the fact that the girl probably had a tape recorder hidden in her bulky handbag. 'People have been dying since the dawn of time and yet it is one of the things we know surprisingly little about. Everyone has grown excited about the possibility of extending their normal lifespan, of the use of prosthetics and transplants, of chemicals to reduce the physical effects of the aging process, and yet they all seem to overlook the obvious. Death is a physical reality. By studying it we may be able to learn something about it and, by so doing, find means to make it easier, less terrifying and more acceptable.'

Quietly she said, 'But isn't that the job of organized religion?'

'Perhaps, and for those who have faith religion can provide a great comfort. But we live in a world of diminishing faith and, in any case, science must find its own answers. What happens to a man when he dies? We know that there are five emotional stages on the normal path to final dissolution: the first is denial — 'It can't be happening to me'; the second is anger — 'Why should this be happening to me?'; the third is desperation — 'I'll do anything if only I can live!' . . . then comes increasing depression — 'What's the good of trying?'; and, finally, acceptance — 'Let's get it over'.'

'And you hope to do something about that?'

'We've done something about it,' he corrected. 'At least, Professor Denislov has evolved a technique which has tremendous implications. But more of that later. Now, I suppose, you want to look over the Institute?'

'Please.'

He finished his coffee. 'Right. Then let's get at it.'

* * *

The wards were long, wide, well-lit and bright with gleaming paint yet, even so, they held an intangible something which plucked at the nerves and induced depression. Sue shivered as they walked past the rows of beds each with its silent occupant. From the pillows mask-like faces stared at the ceiling, the eyes dull, incurious even when she halted and stared at them.

Kelough said quietly, 'In this ward we have the old and mostly senile. With the majority communication is almost impossible. They are in the final emotional state and very close to termination.'

'Termination? Don't you mean death?'

'By many standards these people are already dead. They breathe and their hearts continue to beat but, mentally, they are vegetables.' He caught her arm and led her down the ward. 'Please do not get emotional. These people are going to die whether they are here or elsewhere. We have others, those who are in the terminal stages of incurable diseases, and they are younger and better able to communicate. Even so they know they are going to die. Here we make no attempt at pretence.'

She took a deep breath as they left the ward. 'Tell me, Doctor, how do you find people willing to work here?'

'You think of them as ghouls?'

'I think they must love death to want to be so close to it.'

'An emotional reaction of which you should be ashamed,' he said sharply.

'People die, they do it all the time, what you have seen is nothing special. We provide comfort and aid in the final hours — are you going to blame us for that?'

'No,' she said slowly, 'but there is something else. Rumour has it that many of those who work here are promiscuous. They — '

'Rumour,' he interrupted bitterly. 'Take any group of people and any accusation you wish to make will probably be true in one or more cases. But it is equally true that working here presents an emotional hazard. The staff tend to compensate exactly as do morticians, interns and ambulance attendants. Graveyard humour is a safety valve. When people are too closely associated with suffering and death they either become detached or insane. Here the staff are consistently reminded of their own mortality and they tend to live a little harder as a result.'

He led the way into a passage flanked with closed doors. One of them opened as they approached and a middle-aged woman wearing rusty black with a string of coral beads around her neck stepped into the passage. She had been crying, her cheeks still wet with tears.

Gently Kelough said, 'A bad one, Mrs. Blight?'

'He was so afraid,' she said. 'So terribly afraid.'

'And?'

She shook her head, diving into a pocket for a handkerchief as she walked away. Kelough glanced at the girl.

'Mrs. Blight is a telepathist and a good one. She tries to maintain contact with the mind. Sometimes it isn't easy.'

'Contact? You mean beyond death?'

'Yes.' Kelough paused at another door. He opened it and they looked inside. An old woman lay on a hospital cot. To one side of her sat a doctor-nurse, at the other an elderly man with a prominent paunch and sagging jowls. He smiled, perfectly calm and relaxed.

'You're a little early, Doctor,' he said in a smooth, deep voice. 'Our friend isn't yet ready to pass over. It will be another thirty minutes at least before I enter a trance and arrange for a guide.'

'Mr. Grenshaw,' explained Kelough as

201

they continued down the passage. 'He's a medium of thirty years standing and with an impeccable reputation.'

'Telepathists,' murmured Sue. 'Mediums. Are you serious?'

'Perfectly serious.'

'But to use such weirdies! I understood that the Institute was run on scientific lines.'

'It is and that is why we use them.' Kelough smiled as he saw her expression. 'You're letting emotional prejudice get in the way again. Our job here is to gather data and we aren't too proud to refuse to consider that, possibly, there are things we do not know. And even negative results can be of value. That is why we welcome the cooperation of anyone who has any claim to specialised knowledge or unusual talents.'

'In order to find proof of an afterlife?'

'In order to discover as many facts as we can,' corrected Kelough patiently. 'We aren't trying to prove anything. We are simply studying what happens when a person dies.'

'And the Capsule?'

Kelough had been waiting for the question. 'Simply an extension of those studies. Would you like to see it in operation?'

★   ★   ★

In the Capsule a man lay dying. He was eighty-two years of age and had been senile for ten. Completely nude he lay beneath the searching glare of lights, an assembly of withered skin, knotted veins and wasted tissue. A mass of wires sprouted from his shaven skull, more from the region of his heart and lungs, the electronic tendrils connected to a mechanism beneath the pallet. The bed itself was a sheet of inert plastic mounted on a delicate balance. Covering it, enclosing both man and mechanism in a hermetic seal, an elongated bubble of transparent plastic gave the Capsule its name.

'Time?' Professor Somers didn't glance at the recording dials mounted on the wall, concentrating instead on the figure within the transparency. A technician interpreted the question and gave the desired answer.

'Thirty-four minutes since enclosure, sir.'

Somers nodded and stepped back from the Capsule, almost bumping into Kelough where he stood beside Sue. Interestedly she looked around the room. It was filled with apparatus, spidery needles recording on paper rolls — every minute fraction of altered weight, the flow of replenished air, the humidity, heartbeat and respiration. A complex encephalograph took care of the brain emissions and cameras and electronic devices recorded all visual and electro-magnetic phenomena within the enclosed space. Around and about the various instruments white-coated technicians waited for the subject to die.

They were like priests, she thought, administering the Last Rites, or rather they were vultures waiting to see what they could snatch at the last moment. No material or force known to science could enter or leave the Capsule unrecorded. If there was such a thing as a soul and if that thing had material or electro-magnetic substance they would plot its passing.

'Respiration uneven,' said a technician quietly. 'Heart failing.'

Unconsciously the observers edged closer. In the bright lights, pathetic in his nudity, the subject lay waiting for his final moment. They were all waiting. For a moment Sue wondered what they would do if, by some miracle, the old man should find a sudden urge to live. If, by some magic of will, he could beat away the advancing dissolution.

Kill him? Let gas enter the Capsule? Send a bolt of current through the wires?

It was too fanciful a notion for even a reporter to entertain and she dismissed it, annoyed with herself for her loss of detachment. This was merely a scientific experiment, a controlled attempt to answer the question that had plagued Mankind since the dawn of time. What happened at the moment of death? Did something immaterial leave the body? What happened to the ego when the mechanism died?

'Dissolution approaching,' said the

technician. His voice was as dispassionate as if he were talking of a failing engine.

Sue felt a sudden constriction of the stomach. She had never been so close to death before and, despite the inhumanity of the surroundings, she responded to a primitive awe. From a speaker came the relayed sound of the death-rattle trapped phlegm caught in the trachea, horrible in its implications.

A strobelight began to wink with eye-scorching brilliance. On the bed the figure stirred, the eyes opening, one hand lifting towards the wires trailing from the skull. It fell as the lips parted in the final rictus.

'Termination completed,' the technician. 'Now entering the final cycle.'

It would last for fifteen minutes, a scientific wake, for who could be certain as to the exact moment of death? A healthy subject could be revived after termination. The heart could be made to beat again, the lungs suck air, and if it were done quickly enough there was no apparent harm. Only when the brain was disintegrating from lack of oxygen could the subject be said to have finally terminated.

★　★　★

Sue emptied the glass, shuddered and said, 'Thanks, I needed that.'

'French brandy, reporters, for the use of.' Kelough watched as the colour returned to her cheeks. 'Are you all right now?'

'Yes.' Sue drew a deep breath as Kelough handed her a cigarette. 'I'm sorry about that. I didn't think I was the fainting kind.'

'You didn't faint. You got a little queasy, that's all.' He lit the cigarette and watched as she blew smoke. They were back in his office and he could still feel the soft impact of her curves as he'd half carried her from the Capsule. 'It happens all the time. Even nurses sometimes faint at the sight of blood.'

'You're being kind. It's just that I've never seen anyone die before. At first it didn't seem real — and then, suddenly, it hit me. That was a real man in there and he had really died. And for what?'

'That is a question no one can answer.'

She was suddenly irritable. 'I don't mean why he died — I mean why was he made to do it in that way? A specimen to be probed and checked, measured and weighed. Couldn't he have been allowed to die quietly in dignity and peace?'

'You're getting emotional again,' he said. 'Science is the business of asking questions, and if some of these aren't pleasant, it can't be helped. He was going to die. Nothing could have saved him. Was it wrong to try and learn something from his passing?'

'But — '

'You're not a fool!' he snapped, responding to her own irritation. 'You know that in every teaching hospital patients are expected to cooperate with the interns. You know too that many of them are used as guinea-pigs to determine the value of new drugs and methods of treatment. How else can medical science advance? Yet, when it comes to us watching a man die, you protest. For Heaven's sake be reasonable.'

'See it my way,' she said.

'What?'

'Be reasonable — see it my way.' She crushed out her cigarette. 'It's a joke, forget it. And you're right. I am being illogical, but that's probably because I'm a woman. Even so it seems to me that you are chasing the end of the rainbow. What happens to a person when they die? It's a good question but isn't it like asking what happens to the flame of a candle when it's blown out?'

'A good analogy,' said Kelough, 'even though not wholly exact.' He sat down and looked up at Sue where she perched on the edge of his desk. 'In the old days people believed that the body consisted of three parts; the body, the brain and a thing they termed a soul. It had various names, for example the Egyptians called it the Ka, but all basically meant the same. The essence of a man, his individuality, his ego, is assumed to acquire a separate existence after death. Freed of the body it went to Heaven, or Valhalla, or somewhere similar depending on the particular religion and culture. The point is that people were firmly convinced that the ego continued after death.'

'So?'

'We grew cynical, or mechanistic, or practical, call it what you like. The existence of the soul was discounted and we assumed that everything could be answered by the interaction of the brain and the body. We learned that one could influence the other and maintained belief in the existence of the soul became an article of faith. Oh, people still professed a belief in an afterlife but it was a desperate hope rather than a strong conviction. And then we began to learn a little more. We discovered, for example, that reality could be altered. A subject in deep hypnosis told that he would not experience pain literally did not experience pain. I don't mean that he didn't feel it, I mean that the biological reaction attendant on the stimulus we call pain was demonstrably absent. He did not feel pain because it did not exist.'

'I remember those experiments,' said Sue. 'At least I read about them. They did some pretty weird things, telling a subject that something didn't exist, telling him that something which didn't did, altering the colour-conception, a lot of things.'

'And each experiment was controlled and checked by physical and mental recordings.' Kelough leaned back in his chair. 'I'll make it short. It was discovered that the body has what can only be described as a life of its own. A functional system, rather, which when left alone will operate at a high level of efficiency. The brain is almost similar in that it works as a guidance system for the body, a computer if you like. But what of the third element, the mind?'

'Are you saying that you have proved the existence of the soul?'

'No. The results from the Capsule have so far been negative in that we cannot discover any emission from the body at the moment of, or after, death. But we do know that the brain continues to live after the body has ceased to function. The encephalograph proves that. The point is, what happens to the ego after the body has died?'

'The sixty-four billion dollar question,'

she said drily. 'You have the answer?'

'Yes,' he said. 'At least Professor Denislov thinks so.'

* * *

The woman could not have been more than forty-five years of age. She lay supine on the bed, her head on the pillow, eyes closed and chest rising in the rhythm of sleep. Her arms were above the covers, hands slightly curved, the nails trimmed and neat. Each bicep bore a plastic collar, a sterile tube in both embedded in major arteries, their openings sealed. Other tubes snaked from beneath the covers and carried, Sue guessed, waste products.

'Linda Hawkson,' said Kelough. 'She is in the final stages of multiple sclerosis. Termination could be from two to five months if she follows the normal pattern.' He moved to another bed lower down the small ward. This one held a man. Like the woman he rested quietly and his biceps also bore the plastic collars. 'Fred Cullen, thirty-eight, a steel worker. He has extensive carcinoma of the liver, spleen

212

and bowels. Awake he would be in constant agony and would need continuous sedation. He has been here two months and should have terminated a week ago.'

'Should have?'

'If the prognosis is to be trusted, yes. It is our belief that the Denislov Technique actually enables the subject to extend the expected lifespan as well as removing all fear and anxiety from the terminal stages. Perhaps the extension is directly due to that single factor — though as yet it is a little too early to be positive.'

Kelough moved on down the ward. 'Charles Armitage,' he murmured. 'Sheila Mayhew. Dennis Tucker. Maria Ariosto. Eve Baker . . . ' There were fifteen of them. All dying. All, apparently, completely at rest in normal sleep.

'You've drugged them,' accused Sue.

'No, at least not in the way you're thinking of. They did receive initial tranquilization together with certain hypnotic derivatives but that is all. They are not under sedation. They were hypnotized,' he explained. 'Thrown into a deep trance and conditioned to feel no pain. The rest is due to the Denislov Technique.'

He stepped aside as attendants entered the ward. They pulled a trolley before them, the vehicle bearing a mass of complicated apparatus. Sue watched as they halted beside one of the beds and connected plastic tubes to the collars and biceps.

'Intravenous feeding?'

'Basically, yes,' said Kelough. 'At present necessary though we hope later to be able to divorce a section of the brain so that the subject will be able to feed himself and perform necessary functions without artificial aid. You realize what the technique does, of course.'

'Yes, Bren — ' She broke off and continued. 'Our informant explained that. You have short-circuited the brain. In effect you have turned these people into mindless, brainless vegetables.'

So it had been Brenner. Kelough scowled at the disloyalty while understanding it. Denislov had been savagely hurtful when firing the man. It was to be expected that he had tried to seek revenge and he had, obviously, preconditioned the girl to expect the worst. Her snap judgment proved that.

Patiently he said, 'Wrong again. Everyone of these people is enjoying a full and active life. Subjective, of course. But none the less real. We know it is real for the lives they are living are their own.'

'More hypnotism?'

'No. Let me draw an analogy. Imagine a phonograph record, an extremely long-player, one so long that the single groove covers the events of an entire lifetime from birth to the present. Now think of the needle. The Denislov technique picks it up and sets it down again close to the beginning. We aim for a point fifteen years after birth — there is no reason for subjecting the patient to the usual anguish of early childhood. Now imagine the player to be speeded up so that the record which has taken a lifetime to cut is played over in a matter of minutes.'

He gestured towards the silent figures on the beds.

'That is what is happening to them. Instead of lying here, in pain, terrified of the coming extinction of termination, they are reliving their own past.'

'For how long?' Sue frowned as she thought of an objection. 'What happens when they come out of it?'

'They don't. They live up to the time when they were thrown back — and then they are thrown back. A continuous, repetitive cycle. It will continue until final termination.'

'And then?'

'And then, we think, it happens all over again — but in reverse.'

He smiled at her baffled expression. 'It's logical when you think about it. As a computer the brain has been storing data all through its existence. Everything you see, have felt, have learned and experienced, is all there. Death comes, the body ceases to function but the brain, the computer, remains viable for minutes longer. While it does so the ego remains intact. Then the brain begins to disintegrate. We think, and there is evidence to show, that there is a moment when the stored data is erased. The record player begins to spin backwards in a sudden discharge of energy. The result can only be a retrospective repetition of the events of a lifetime.'

'In a split second?'

'Subjective time has no limitations.'

'But backwards?' She frowned, thinking. 'They would know. The people who die, I mean. And how can anyone live backwards?'

'Every moment of your life you are seeing things upside down,' he pointed out. 'You don't realize it because your brain corrects the image. And how would you know that you are living backwards? As far as you are concerned the future doesn't exist and that would apply either because you hadn't lived it yet or because the memory of it has been erased. But you remember the past because that remains. And don't forget that awareness is a matter of split-second repetition. You are aware now — but as soon as you even think of it that now has gone to be replaced by another.'

She stood thoughtful, watching as the

trolley with its attendants moved from one bed to another, trying to imagine what it must be like to relive a life over and over again, to make the same mistakes, to feel the same pains. The anguish, despair, hurt and loss. But to know again the pleasures and excitement, the anticipation and joy. It was a futile speculation. They could not know that what they experienced was a repetition. They had no way of telling.

'Sue?'

She turned to face Kelough and felt again the odd sensation she had experienced in the office when first they had met. A conviction that she had stood here before, knowing, somehow, the trolley would veer to the left, that he would step forward, one hand lifted as if to touch her as he asked if he could see her again. A moment which passed.

'Yes,' she said. 'That would be nice.' Then, as she saw his blank expression, added, quickly, 'I'm sorry. It just happened again. That thing, déjà vu, you called it?'

'You answered me. I hadn't spoken.'

'I thought you had.'

He shook his head. 'That's odd, but never mind. We'll talk about it. Anything else you'd like to see?'

'Something I'd like to know.' She gestured towards the beds. 'If what you say is right how would we ever know we aren't like one of those? Or that we had died and — ?'

Kelough shrugged. 'We wouldn't.'

THE END

NEW CASES FOR DOCTOR MORELLE

Ernest Dudley

Young heiress Cynthia Mason lives with her violent stepfather, Samuel Kimber, the controller of her fortune — until she marries. So when she becomes engaged to Peter Lorrimer, she fears Kimber's reaction. Peter, due to call and take her away, talks to Kimber in his study. Meanwhile, Cynthia has tiptoed downstairs and gone — she's vanished without trace. Her friend Miss Frayle, secretary to the criminologist Dr. Morelle, tries to find her — and finds herself a target for murder!

THE EVIL BELOW

Richard A. Lupoff

'Investigator seeks secretary, amanuensis, and general assistant. Applicant must exhibit courage, strength, willingness to take risks and explore the unknown . . . ' In 1905, John O'Leary had newly arrived in San Francisco. Looking for work, he had answered the advert, little understanding what was required for the post — he'd try anything once. In America he found a world of excitement and danger . . . and working for Abraham ben Zaccheus, San Francisco's most famous psychic detective, there was never a dull moment . . .

A STORM IN A TEACUP

Geraldine Ryan

In the first of four stories of mystery and intrigue, *A Storm in a Teacup*, Kerry has taken over the running of her aunt's café. After quitting her lousy job and equally lousy relationship with Craig, it seemed the perfect antidote. But her chef, with problems of his own, disrupts the smooth running of the café. Then, 'food inspectors' arrive, and vanish with the week's takings. But Kerry remembers something important about the voice of one of the bogus inspectors . . .

SÉANCE OF TERROR

Sydney J. Bounds

Chalmers decides to attend one of Dr. Lanson's nightly séances because it's somewhere warm to rest his weary feet. A decision he regrets when a luminous cloud forms above the assembled people. Strangely, from the cloud comes a warning: someone there is about to die to prevent them from revealing secrets. A man defiantly leaps to his feet, the lights are extinguished, the man's voice is cut off and an ear-piercing shriek reverberates around the room . . .